A
DEEP
DISTURBANCE

Also by Constance Rauch

The Landlady
The Spy on Riverside Drive

A DEEP DISTURBANCE

CONSTANCE RAUCH

A·THOMAS·DUNNE BOOK

ST. MARTIN'S PRESS
NEW YORK

Design by Glen M. Edelstein

Library of Congress Cataloging-in-Publication Data

Rauch, Constance.
    A deep disturbance / by Constance Rauch.
        p.   cm.
    "A Thomas Dunne book."
    ISBN 0-312-04682-0
    I. Title.
    PS3568.A788D4   1990
    813'.54—dc20   90-37314
                                                                 CIP

First Edition: November 1990

10 9 8 7 6 5 4 3 2 1

For
Senta Kauffeldt Weil,
in loving memory

CHAPTER

1

ALL she could think to do was grab the children and run. Time enough later for lawyers . . . for courts of law . . . for police? Yes. Probably there would have to be police.

But not now. Now she would whisk her precious, perfect little girls away. Far, far away. As though she might yet prevent . . . protect them . . . from what had manifestly already been done to them.

Some terrible damage had been done. Had to have been. The pictures made that quite plain. Innocent little faces rouged into grotesque hoydenish masks . . . babyish bodies posed and displayed for . . . for . . . No! For *nobody*! Ever.

Stabbed again by all the horror of that first moment, she shuddered and pushed the images into some black corner of her mind. If the three of them were going to get through this, she would have to keep her attention on the road. They were approaching the thruway tollbooth.

"Let me put the money in! Let me! It's my turn!"

"Sorry, Libby, this is the kind where you get a ticket and pay at the very end."

1

"Aww. That's no fun."

"Well, maybe so, but you can hold the ticket for me if you like. As long as you promise to take good care of it. Okay?"

The tollbooth attendant saw nothing unusual or remarkable about the pretty, preoccupied young woman with the two small daughters squirming and jumping about excitedly in the backseat. It was a lovely morning in May, the Thursday before Memorial Day.

Bet she's taking the second car up to the country place, the attendant thought, a bit enviously, because she was no longer young and her children had grown and gone. Opening it up for the summer, getting it ready for Daddy. And who would Daddy be? she wondered. Probably a dentist or a stockbroker. A good provider, in any case.

"There you are, dear. Have a good trip, now."

"Thank you," Madeleine Rafferty said cheerfully enough, pulling away, her spirits unaccountably lifting. As she stepped on the accelerator and rolled the car window back up, she said to the eight-year-old Libby, "You can read the names of the places printed on the back, if you want, and find out how much we'll need to pay when we get to our exit."

"How far?"

"All the way to Albany."

"Albany? Is that where we're going? I thought you said we were going to Indian Meadow, in the mountains."

"We are. Albany is where we change highways. We get on the Northway—that takes us right up through the Adirondack Mountains."

"Golly, we're going to be cooped up in this dumb car for days and days," said Tillie, the five-year-old.

"No, honey, just most of today. It's going to be fun. You'll see. There are some really neat things along the way." However specious and transient the sensation might be, for a moment there it had felt as though they actually were taking a vacation trip. Hold on to that brave thought,

2

little lady, Madeleine murmured to herself, taking clinical note of her evident progress from despair to a more-or-less healthy mordancy.

"Can we stop and eat soon?"

"How about waiting another hour, okay?"

"But I'm *starving.*" Tillie insisted.

"Fine, just open up your lunch box, then. I packed goodies for each of you."

Libby pounced on one of Tillie's cookies, provoking another of their everyday battles for supremacy. It didn't seem to matter that she had the very same cookies in her own lunch box. It wasn't serious; Madeleine let her mind drift away. There was a lot of thinking that needed doing . . . provided she could avoid the unthinkable.

God! What if she'd actually killed him! He'd been lying there on the floor so gray and still. . . . What good would she have been to the children then?

No. No to all that. That was then. This was now. Today. The next six months.

Amazing she'd found somebody to sublet the apartment for six months, just like that. A divorced man, retreating back to the city from the smoking ruins of a marriage in Mamaroneck. He'd even offered an extra two months' rent to clinch the deal. What if he wrecked the place? Threw wild parties? Dealt drugs? Madeleine didn't care. She'd taken the money and run. All the way to the Adirondacks.

The place she was renting in the tiny hamlet of Indian Meadow had also become available because its owners were splitting up. While lawyers wrangled over who got the rights to the house, it had been offered for rent. No lease required. Indeed, judging by how excited the broker had sounded on the phone, finding a tenant for six whole months—June through October—was apparently quite a coup up there. Indian Meadow was not a thriving vacation resort. Renters probably came in dribs and drabs: one week here, ten days there, and lots of empty spaces in between. But it would be perfect for her and the girls. Madeleine just knew it. How could Gil possibly ever find them way up there?

She now had six months to establish a new life . . . all because of something her boss, Matthew Blaustein, bless him, had casually mentioned to her some months before.

"You know, Madeleine, we're always looking for new authors to do romances for us. Have you ever considered taking a stab at it?" Matt held up his hand to prevent her from making the flippant, derogatory remark he could see forming on her rather transparent face.

"Don't say it. I'm not asking you to sell your soul to the devil. Hear me out. We're starting a new program here at Dexter, Inc., which if it works will make me quite a hero, because it will save us a bundle. Which is simply to pay some writers regular salaries. Think you could turn out two romances a year for us, Maddie?"

The question caught her off guard. She looked at her boss incredulously and blurted out, "Betcha I could. But, Matt, I'm an *editor,* and a good one, I like to think. Why should I even consider a thing like that?"

"Forty thou and all the same bennies you get now, Maddie, my girl. Think about it."

"Wow. You mean if I could deliver two decent, saleable titles a year, that'd be . . ."

"Forty thou plus a year."

"My God, what makes you think I could do it? I mean, really?" Maddie asked, tempted in spite of herself. Her salary as junior editor was thirty-two five.

"I've seen your work. Half of Serena Rinaldi's book is really you. You're a natural storyteller."

"Matt, you flatter me. I guess. At least I'm flattered by your faith in me, if not by the choice of genre. Anyway, what I really hope to become, more than anything, is a senior editor at some really good hardcover house . . . you know that. Sure, the money isn't all that good at first, but in time . . ."

4

"Dream on, kid. But don't forget the offer. It's good for a while yet—at least until they fire me. Think about it. You could work at home, take better care of your girls . . . might even be better for you and Gil . . ."

"Matt, I take very good care of my girls, thank you." And I take excellent care of Gil, too, dammit, she'd said to herself. "I will think about it. Thanks for telling me. Now, about your promotion plan for the Schaeffer book . . ." And that had been that. Madeleine had hardly remembered the offer again.

Until yesterday . . . when she'd taken him up on it.

As the highway cut through sharp and majestic mountain passes and they became progessively more removed from their former world, Madeleine willingly gave herself up to the illusion that this was simply a vacation. If that's what it took to get herself through this, she would become a vacationer with a vengeance. Just watch her.

Even Libby and Tillie caught the feeling. They'd finally let go of their urban querulousness and were sitting together companionably in the backseat.

"Wow, look at that! Let's pull over, Mom. I want to see how far you can see."

"Well, okay, why not?" Madeleine slowed down and pulled over to the parking area. They got out and sat down together on a low granite wall from which they could see mile upon mile of hills and valleys, rolling off into a filmy blue haze. Farms, houses, small villages, fields newly planted and trees newly green or in fragrant blossom . . . greens, yellows, delicate pinks. They watched in awe as a pair of hawks described a silent, proprietary circle high above their heads.

Intent, Libby adjusted the bright red frames of the round-eyed glasses resting on the bridge of her perfect nose. She didn't want to miss a thing. For once, Tillie's quick mouth was stilled. Maddie watched her alert little face absorb the many wonders stretched out before them.

"Isn't this *great*, Mom?"

"Are you glad now that we came?"

"Yeah! This is fun!"

They stayed for a few minutes, gazing dreamily across the Hudson far below them, and way beyond it to the foothills of the Berkshires. To Maddie, the view seemed after a time to taunt her with the possibility of a kind of radiant, perfect happiness that simply *was* . . . that one didn't have to work for every minute. Surely there had to be something like that, somewhere . . . even if she'd never experienced it personally.

She looked out over the houses spread out in the valley below, tiny in the distance, and wondered how many of them contained well-thumbed copies of Dexter Romances. She didn't have a single idea, standing there, as to how she would go about actually writing one.

A cloud passed over the sun and the temperature immediately went down. Libby hugged her arms and said, "Brrr!"

"Yes, well, we're up at a pretty high elevation here, you know. It's cooler than down in the valleys. Let's get back in the car, shall we?" They tumbled in happily, burrowing among their pillows, welcoming the cozy warmth of their rumpled familiar belongings. Secure within the comforts of this home away from home, the little group had solidified imperceptibly into a new unit: Mommy, Libby, and Tillie.

Daddy had been dropped.

Nearly four hours later, the car was whining slowly uphill in low gear. As the narrow dirt road followed a rough stone wall covered with brambles and honeysuckle, the three of them were singing lustily and out of tune: *This old man, he played three, he played knick-knack on his knee.*

At last they came to some rutted tire tracks that indicated a rudimentary driveway. There was a mailbox on a post, a broad, mowed field of some several acres sloping gently uphill, and, set smack in the middle of it, the big old house that was going to be their new home.

6

The quiet was uncanny.

They were halfway up a mountain, and the altitude freshened the air. Although there was no wind to speak of, the bright green leaves on the trees rustled continuously, and the long grass in the meadow rippled in successive waves. The loudest sound was that of birds—the clear, liquid notes of robins dominating a thrumming, chirping chorus of sparrows and grackles and red-winged blackbirds. The grass around the house was freshly cut, and the clean smell of it mingled with that of damp woodland earth, of sun-warmed pine, and of honeysuckle just coming into bloom for the first time.

It was heaven.

Her legs somewhat unsteady from the long drive, Madeleine let her car door slam behind her and made her way to the mailbox, which bore the name PERRY, as she had been told it would. She opened it and withdrew a manila envelope marked:

TO: Madeleine Rafferty

FROM: Joseph P. Mitford, Lakeshore Realty

Inside were several keys on a ring and several pages of typewritten instructions regarding the Perry house bound in a blue report folder. A personal note was attached to the cover with a paper clip. It was written in a round, easy-to-read hand and said, simply, "Welcome to Indian Meadow. We hope you will enjoy your stay." It was signed "Joe Mitford." That had been the man she'd dealt with on the phone.

The girls had already run up to the house and were skittering about the broad front porch, waiting for her to let them in. Grinning broadly, she ran across the grass and scampered up the porch steps to join them.

They stepped into the house, holding hands, and stopped just inside the front door. They were in a small entranceway, hardly as big as a closet, done up in faded flower-sprigged wallpaper. A steep stairway rose up almost directly in front of them. There was a gentle old house smell: wood and plaster, board and batten, wood smoke and kerosene, and generations of camphor-stored belongings. Madeleine felt herself going back to a simpler, older time and place.

"Oh, will you look at this house!" she said, moving from the entranceway into the spacious sitting room to the left of it. It was furnished with a shabby-genteel assortment of mismatched furniture, slipcovered with faded floral prints in which rose, maroon, and deep green predominated. Beautiful old Indian blankets graced the backs of some of these pieces. The big rag rug that covered the floor had in turn been covered—at strategic points of wear—with boldly patterned Indian scatter rugs.

The late-afternoon sun pouring in through the old bubbly glass windowpanes made everything glow with a gemlike warmth. The interior wall was made of logs—evidently part of the original mountain cabin around which the rest of the house had grown over the years. Yes, there were the two original log cabin windows—converted into shelves and filled with typical Adirondack artifacts: grass, willow, and split-wood baskets, a miniature canoe paddle, a pair of snowshoes, old scenic views in intricate twig frames. A massive raised stone fireplace straddled the far corner of the room.

There was an old mantel clock above the fireplace. Curious to see whether it worked, Madeleine opened the little door in the clockface and found a tiny key. She set the delicate hands at the time on to her wristwatch and slowly, carefully, turned the key several times. The clock began to tick: a ponderous, mellow, comforting sound. It seemed a brave and auspicious gesture. Madeleine had now officially taken up residence . . . and she was in command.

Tillie and Libby had already darted through what had obviously been the original cabin door, which now led to the kitchen–cum–dining room. Madeleine joined them. She saw a black cast-iron gas range perched on a brick pedestal, a claw-footed bathtub that did double-duty as counter space beneath its wide, hinged wooden cover, and a big double sink. Madeleine tried the faucets; hot and cold water poured obediently forth. *Good!* She looked around, approvingly, admiring the soft cream tongue-and-groove walls and the way the hardware—hinges, door pulls, latches, claw feet—had neatly been picked out in a deep barn red. Though the arrangement of the room's parts might have seemed whimsical and impractical to some, it felt just right to Madeleine. There was a lot more to a good kitchen than so many yards of seamless Formica.

The heart of this large room—once the entire mountain cabin—was dominated by an oval table that might easily seat a dozen. Its surface had been nicked and scratched and bleached almost white by more than a century's worth of scrubbing. This was a table that had endured generations of family meals, celebrations, crises. Maybe even a wake or two. They would have laid out the dearly departed right on top of it.

Tillie went to the table and happily surveyed the eccentric collection of chairs assembled around it. Then she pulled out a high, ladderback model with a rush seat and grandly sat down in it.

"This will be *my* place!" she announced.

Libby chose a chair of her own on the other side of the table and also sat. Madeleine laughed.

"Well, I guess I'd better take this one before anybody else does!" Sitting there at the head of the mellow oval table, looking across it to her two little girls, she let out a sigh of relief. It was wonderful to see them both looking so fine and happy in spite of everything.

"And Daddy, what about him?" Tillie asked then. "Where will Daddy sit when he gets here?"

Before Madeleine could think of something to reply, Libby, her too-wise eight-year-old, blurted, "Daddy's not coming, Tillie. Ever. Right, Mommy?" Glints of late-afternoon sun flashed in the lenses of Libby's glasses, making it difficult for Madeleine to gauge the expression in her serious gray eyes.

Oh, my poor baby, she thought. How much were you hurt? How can I ever make it up to you?

"You're right, Libby. It's going to be just the three of us. For as long as we stay in Indian Meadow."

"Good," Libby said, clearly relieved.

Tillie said nothing. She just looked at her older sister and gave a slight, tentative nod.

CHAPTER

2

BEYOND the kitchen, they discovered another stairway leading to a hidden-away back bedroom. Two narrow white iron bedsteads covered with pretty patchwork quilts sat cozily beneath the sharply slanting eaves. Low bookshelves and cupboards lined the walls, which some pleasant soul had aptly papered in pink and blue morning glories. The alcove at the head of the stairs even boasted a private little window seat. Libby and Tillie tried the window seat out for size, pronounced it perfect, and promptly claimed this room as their own.

With its broad front porch and peaked overhanging roof, the house looked like a big square Adirondack-style camp. But it was actually shaped like a *T*. In its gradual outward growth from the original log cabin, the front of the house—living room, front bedroom, center stairway and upstairs bedrooms—had come last; in effect, crossing the *T*.

Madeleine chose the downstairs front bedroom because she could picture herself seated at the small maple writing table that stood in front of the windows. There she would be, every evening, in a pool of quiet lamplight—with nothing but the sound of crickets to accompany the diligent scratchings of her pen. She unpacked a sheaf of yellow legal pads, shiny and new in its cellophane wrapping, and placed it hopefully on the desk.

Supper that first night consisted of egg salad sandwiches and Campbell's tomato soup. It was fun getting to know the dishes in the cupboards and the pots and pans by the stove. Old mismatched crockery chronicled America's changing tastes: bits of Depression glass, Fiesta ware, Russell Wright, and lots of F. W. Woolworth's finest.

When Libby and Tillie began to droop, Madeleine went up the stairs with them to their new room. They showed off how they'd put their things away, and she had to admire the contents of each and every dresser drawer, praising the girls lavishly. They really had done a fine job. Very grown up. But now they were so sleepy they needed to be helped into their pajamas like little babies. She could feel the heavy fatigue emanating from them like heat from a fire. They were already asleep; tucking them in and kissing them good-night was a mere formality.

She tidied the kitchen. Turned off the lights. Went to her room. Undressed. Climbed into the high old-fashioned bed now done up in her own fresh Bloomingdale's sheets. Turned off her light and sat back against the pillows, looking out at the dark landscape. Moonlight shone down on the grassy field. A few treetops were discernible against the inky sky. Exhausted as she was, she was afraid to let go. Afraid to sleep. Afraid of what she might dream. She tried to prepare herself with calm, hopeful thoughts . . . to ponder the novel she had come here to write. Maybe she could hit on a character or a setting. . . .

The brain being a complex and mysterious mechanism, this is indeed what she then began to do. Except that, having drifted off within seconds of turning out the light, she was fast asleep at the time.

12

*   *   *

The two Rafferty girls were up and about their new domain—still in their pajamas—before seven. They giggled and shivered deliciously as they watched their bare feet make clear tracks in the dewy grass. They scampered up to the top of the hill and looked down over the house and out beyond it . . . down the mountain and out over the entire nearby range, the colors shading with each successive ridge, from bright, sunlit green to deepest slate blue.

"Look!" Tillie said. "Over *there,* there's a *lake!*"

"Where?" Libby replied cautiously, not daring to believe her.

"*There.* See? You can see water between the trees." Libby crouched down to her five-year-old sister's height and squinted in the general direction of her pointing finger.

"Hey! I think I see it! Wow! A lake! A real lake!"

They went running back to the house, slamming the screen door behind them like a claxon.

"Ma! Ma!" They ran into her room. Madeleine awoke with her heart in her mouth, thinking something terrible had happened.

"There's a *lake!* Come *look!*"

They were both clambering on top of her now, climbing on her rumpled sheets with their wet and grassy feet, leaving a trail of woodland debris. But Madeleine could not find it in her heart to reprimand them. They wore their new outdoorsy smells with such a swagger and it suited them so well. They had gone off exploring and were returning with the glorious spoils of their adventure, dropping the gift of this unsuspected lake at her feet.

"A lake!" She replied, smiling, sitting up in bed, rubbing her eyes, absently fluffing up her hair. "This I've got to see. . . ." She made them put their sneakers on, and their robes, while she did the same. They left the house and followed a dirt path that led past tall pines and out to a small derelict dock.

13

Lake was perhaps too grand a term to describe the body of water they now beheld in full. *Pond* was more like it. But beautiful. A perfect little basin, clear as crystal.

Why hadn't the real estate guy thought to mention this pond? Would she have taken the place sight unseen if she'd known about it? Wouldn't she have hesitated, knowing she'd have to devote that much more time and energy to keeping an eye on the girls with water so near?

Had she acted too quickly? Ah, what the hell, surely it was a wonder they'd got here at all. She'd been in such a desperate state . . . she must have sounded half mad to the man on the phone. As indeed she had been.

"Libby, Tillie, listen carefully. This is a beautiful pond . . . a wonderful pond . . . but we are going to have to follow some strict safety rules. Water can be very dangerous."

"Aw, Mom, we know! We'll be good, honest! But isn't it a *terrific* lake? Don't you just love it?"

"It's terrific. I love it." Madeleine knelt down on the dock and put a hand into the water and was—somewhat perversely—delighted to find it *icy* cold. They walked back to the house and set about fixing a big country breakfast.

While they ate, the girls chattered about plans for their newfound pond—though they insisted on referring to it as "Our Lake."

"Now," Madeleine said as she finally pushed her plate away and poured herself another cup of coffee. "About the pond. At home, you learned about cars and traffic and street kids who try to rob you of your lunch money. Well, here we're going to have to learn about the dangers of living in the woods. We'll write out the rules on a sheet of paper and make a safety poster that we can hang up right here in the kitchen." When Tillie predictably began to whine, Madeleine added hastily, "Even grown-ups have to follow safety rules in the woods, you know."

"You mean like 'Never wander off into the woods alone'?"

14

"Right, Libby! That's an important one. Let's see how many others we can come up with . . ." Madeleine stopped. She thought she heard a car.

"Anybody home?" A man's tenor voice.

Madeleine opened the front door. A medium-sized man was walking up the driveway. He wore khaki pants, a dark plaid shirt, sleeves rolled to the elbows, and a cheerful expression on his round, open face. Madeleine's first response—fear—subsided.

"Hi! Joe Mitford. Thought I'd stop by and make sure you folks got here all right. See if there was anything you needed." By this time, he'd stepped up to the porch and they were shaking hands.

"Madeleine Rafferty," she said. "Yes, we got here and everything's fine, thanks. We've just discovered the pond on the property."

Joe Mitford beamed. He was standing just where he'd been when they shook hands. Madeleine felt him looking at her. She stepped back. Though he was still standing too close for her to feel comfortable about taking a really good look, she had an uneasy sense that there was something about his face that was not quite right.

"So . . . you found Little Quaker Pond, eh? That's great. The first settlers here were Quakers, you know. It's called Little because there's a bigger one a couple of miles up aways." He was looking squarely into her face; and now Madeleine noticed that owing to their peculiarly asymmetrical configuration, his pale blue eyes seemed unable to respond to what they beheld. He continued, "Of course, most folks come up here for Blue Mirror Lake, you know, down in the village." He swallowed, carefully, and took a deep breath. The conversation seemed somehow to be more important than mere small talk, though Madeleine couldn't tell why. One eye peered to the east, the other to the west . . . yet both were earnestly scanning her face. Was that what was meant by the expression "wall-eyed"? Madeleine couldn't recall ever having met anybody with

15

this condition before. "That's got the state beach and lots of facilities, you know. Little Quaker is just a drop in the bucket, you might say. But folks who stay here at the Perry house always enjoy that pond."

"Is that the name of the people who are, er, splitting up, the owners, Perry?"

"Oh, no. This has been the Perry place for generations. The present owners are named Littlefield. Live down in Westport, Connecticut. Or, used to, anyways. He moved to Manhattan. No . . . I guess this'll always be known as the Perry place 'round these parts. Got lots of history attached to it, you know. This house used to be a station on the Underground Railway. Runaway slaves escaping to Canada used to stop off right here."

"Why, that's fascinating. The Underground Railway! Quaker abolitionists! Imagine that." Libby and Tillie had come out on the porch, so Madeleine introduced them to Joe Mitford. He nodded to each in turn, shaking their hands rather formally, after which they escaped down the steps and ran around toward the back of the house to play. Joe watched them depart.

"Your little girls are going to have such a wonderful time here. We sure did when we all were kids."

"You mean here, at the Perry house?"

"Yes. I'm a Perry, myself, you know. On my m-mother's side. We all used to spend summers at this house when we were small. The six of us. My mother had two boys, three girls, and then me. I'm the baby." Big smile. Mitford, balding slightly and with a thickening middle, apparently thought the description a good joke. Now that the girls had disappeared around the back of the house, Madeleine was again the subject of his uneven gaze.

"Now, about our village," he began anew. "There's an IGA grocery, and a café; the post office and the library are right across the street . . . and, um, the nearest actual shopping center is in Lake Placid, about twenty-five miles away."

16

"Well, thank you, Mr. Mitford. That's very helpful."

"Please," he interrupted.

"Yes?"

"Please just call me Joe." His mouth stretched into an especially broad smile, meant to be winning, but marred by the accumulation of excess saliva at its corners. Madeleine felt unkind for noticing.

"Well," she said, "we certainly appreciate your stopping by like this. . . ." Libby and Tillie came squealing around the corner of the house, pulling what appeared to be a small cart between them.

"Ma! Look what we found! Isn't it great? It's a croquet set!"

"So I see!"

"Can you help us set it up?" Libby asked, jumping up and down in her excitement.

"Why, let me have a look at that," Joe said. "Where did you find this, Libby?" Madeleine was impressed that he remembered that this was Libby. Mostly, she'd noticed, people would remember the name without remembering which child it belonged to.

"It was over by the back steps."

"This is a very good set. It should not be left out. The dew will warp it and that would be a shame." He paused for a moment, pondering, apparently, the shame of treating good equipment badly. "Come, let me show you where this belongs. You'll enjoy seeing this, I think. Oh, Mrs. Rafferty . . . could you bring along that ring of keys I left for you?"

"Sure, Joe." And then, almost in spite of herself, she added, "And do please call me Madeleine." She went and got the keys and caught up with them as they walked.

The path they took led to a large gray-shingled barn that had been only partially visible from the house. Joe unlocked the huge double doors and slid them open, and they all trooped in expectantly, inhaling the cool dusky atmosphere. When their eyes had adjusted to the gloom, Joe

17

said, "My family fixed this place up for us kids—long before I was born. A place to play on rainy days and such. My dad had this big department store down in Utica. Got all this stuff wholesale. I think he was just a kid at heart, really, right up to the day he died. That's when Mother sold this place. I was thirteen by then. There's been a bunch of owners since, of course, but not a one of 'em has ever touched this barn. Looks just like it always did."

The barn was filled, quite literally to the rafters, with toys and games and sports equipment.

"This is amazing," Madeleine said quietly.

"I'll show you around." Proudly, he led them down the aisles between tall glass-fronted cabinets . . . obviously fixtures from that long-ago store in Utica. Anything that didn't fit inside the cabinets was stacked neatly in front of them or suspended from the massive beams overhead: Flexible Flyer sleds, snowshoes, old-fashioned wooden skis and poles, bicycles, tricycles, scooters, archery bows, fishing poles, butterfly nets, old patched canvas inflatable rafts, canoe paddles, oars, lacrosse sticks, even fragile, tattered old kites nobody could possibly ever fly again. Never had Madeleine seen a toy store like this!

The store cabinets held board games, card games, puzzles, building toys, chemistry sets, tea sets, train sets. All were in amazingly well-preserved shiny cardboard boxes emblazoned with bold, futuristic graphics from the thirties and forties: skyscrapers, streamlined trains, steamships with funny fat smokestacks, little propeller-driven planes . . . all in the brightest primary colors.

And so many dolls! Madeleine recognized Shirley Temple among them, eighteen inches high and somewhat the worse for wear. A shiny patent-leather suitcase stood at her side, filled to capacity, she imagined, with tiny 1930s coats and dresses. She could hardly wait to unpack them!

Madeleine looked down at her daughters to see how they were responding to this incredible collection. Up until now, they'd simply been filing past in a kind of mute museumlike

18

trance. They didn't seem to grasp that these were *toys* . . . and that they could actually play with them. But they would, soon enough.

They duly paraded past baseball bats and catcher's mitts, tennis racquets, roller skates, ice skates . . . turned a corner and came to a vacant space between an antique wicker baby stroller that contained a marvelous life-sized baby doll, and an old wooden wagon full of building blocks.

"Ah, here's where that croquet set belongs," Joe said. "Please make sure to put it back here when you're thr—" He didn't get to finish.

There was a shrill, ugly scream from behind.

"It's *mine*! I saw it *first*! Gimme it! *Eeek!*" Tillie was clutching the big baby doll—it was upside down, its fine clothing in total disarray—and Libby, unable to snatch it from her, had resorted to the next-best thing: pulling Tillie's hair.

"Give it to me, it's *mine*!" By the time Madeleine was able to separate them, Libby had gotten Tillie into a vicious hammerlock, and the two had tumbled to the floor, kicking and screaming. "I *hate* you!" "You're stupid!" The fine old baby doll lay spread-eagled on the floor next to them—just another casualty.

"*You!* Stand over *here*." Madeleine placed Tillie on her left. "And, *you*! You stand over *there*!" Libby shuffled sullenly to Madeleine's right. "Now, don't either of you move!" Madeleine bent down, picked up the doll, brushed it off, and deposited it back into the stroller. She turned apologetically to Joe Mitford. "I'm sorry, Joe. They get that way sometimes." Her daughters, their faces red and smudged and tear-stained, looked hateful and altogether unrepentant. Libby wiped her nose and adjusted her glasses with a single careless swipe of the back of her hand. "I want you two to apologize to Mr. Mitford . . . *now!*" Grudgingly, they mumbled something unintelligible.

"Oh, that's quite all right." Joe said. "I know what it's like. Remember, I had sisters, too! They'd fight all the

19

time. Used to just about *kill* each other!" He shook his head, remembering.

"But you know, that doll shouldn't have been out of its cabinet in the first place. Dunno how it came to be sitting in the buggy like that. Can't leave things like this out, you know; if moths don't get 'em, mildew or mice will in no time up here." He opened up the stout old cabinet and tenderly placed the doll behind closed doors. "Look at how snug these doors still fit, after all these years! They sure don't build 'em like this anymore, that's for sure."

They moved on, passing some ladderlike steps leading up to a small hayloft. They went through a broad space that held only some old chairs and a big green Ping-Pong table. And then there were the wide double doors again . . . they'd made a complete circuit. Surprised by the honeyed sunlight, the green smell of grass, they stepped outside.

"Well, I certainly thank you for showing us that wonderful barn! And I do apologize for Libby and Tillie's behavior."

"Oh, that's all right, I enjoyed myself. I don't seem to get out here all that much anymore. Gosh, but we used to have such good times all those years ago!" He chuckled.

Libby and Tillie ran on ahead, back to the croquet set, their quarrel already forgotten.

Joe headed for his car. Then he stopped, slapping his forehead. "I almost went off without telling you." He turned and walked back unhurriedly to join Madeleine on the porch steps.

"There was a message left for you." He reached into the pocket of his plaid shirt and withdrew a pink telephone-message slip. "I guess your phone won't be connected for a few days yet, on account of the holiday weekend and all." He handed the slip to her.

Matt Blaustein was the only person who knew where she was. She'd given him the name of Lakeshore Realty just in case—and that only after she swore him to absolute secrecy. She took the slip from Joe Mitford, wondering what

Matt might have neglected to tell her during the rush of her sudden, unexpected, and never fully explained departure.

She watched Joe's aging Volvo turn down the road and give a cheerful toot of its horn, and then she unfolded the pink slip. It was dated Thursday, five-thirty P.M. Just about the time they'd arrived.

TO: Madeleine Rafferty

FROM: Matt Blaustein

*Gil was here looking you. Please contact
him immediately.*

She read it over again, slowly, as though there'd be some clue hidden between the lines. Her heart was pounding dreadfully. Stupid! Nothing would happen. They were perfectly safe.

Just as long as Matt kept his mouth shut.

Yet as soon as she stepped back into the house, she burst into uncontrollable tears.

At least Libby and Tillie were safely outside and unable to see her.

CHAPTER

3

EVERYTHING had become real again.

Of course there had been clues; long before that final, horrible scene. She knew Gil was drinking. She even knew he used cocaine. That's why they were virtually separated. But she'd been stretched so hard . . . working full-time, raising Libby and Tillie, coping with each day's list of demands, one at a time, until she fell to bed exhausted. If she'd failed to grasp the severity of his disturbance, it was because she was still so dependent on his one remaining contribution to the family.

Twice a week, Gil took care of the girls at his studio after school until it was time to take them home to her.

And then, last Monday night before bedtime, while Madeleine was laying out Libby and Tillie's clothes for them, going over their schedule for the next day, Libby screamed. Screamed!

Madeleine had been telling the girls Daddy would be picking them up as usual after school tomorrow. Libby put her hands over her ears as though she couldn't bear to hear it. Then she let out that shrill, blood-curdling yell, apparently to drown out Madeleine's words.

"No!" she cried. "No! I'm not going there again, ever! You can't make me."

Tillie, pale, her eyes darker and wider than Madeleine had ever seen them, looked over at her sister in uncomprehending horror.

Madeleine calmed Libby down. But all she got out of her was that she hated the studio. It was a yucky place. She hated it. Hated Daddy. And she was never posing for any of his stupid, yucky pictures again.

Madeleine juggled their next day's after-school schedule, finding a neighbor for them to stay with. Then she arranged to leave work early and arrived at Gil's studio unannounced.

She let herself in with her own key. The place looked different to her: seedy, on the skids. It was the first time in months she'd actually been inside. Of course, Gil had taken to spending most nights there. A stale smell of take-out pizza hung in the air. Sure enough, there was the big greasy box, stuck in the wastebasket, its dried-up contents dribbling over the edge, a well-established army of cockroaches busily in attendance.

The darkroom light wasn't on. Gil was nowhere to be seen. She knew her way about the studio all too well. It was where they had met twelve years before, when she'd been on assignment for a trade magazine, and Gilbert Rafferty had been the hottest young photographer in town.

They'd got on so well together, he'd up and asked her to become his assistant. Utterly dazzled by his charm and apparent brilliance, Madeleine accepted. There was never a moment's doubt that far more than a mere assistanceship was at stake. Remembering those amazing innocent early days, Madeleine's focus momentarily softened. Idly, she began to rummage among the plastic photo sleeves littering his desk.

Her eyes were caught by the cruel image of a child—a

little girl—posed in a terrible way. Two little girls. Surely Gil couldn't have stooped to . . . wouldn't be caught dead even *owning* this kind of . . . And then she grasped that the obscenities in front of her were pictures of her own two beloved children. *His* own little girls! How could he possibly . . . What kind of man could possibly . . .

That was when Gil walked through the door with a big warm bag from Burger King in his hand.

"Madeleine!" he said, smiling. "This is a surprise . . ."

Speechless, she held up the prints she'd just found for him to see.

"It isn't what you think, Madeleine. There's nothing there to get upset over. Really. A lot of that's montage, you know. They never saw the male models. I swear . . ."

He was smiling winningly at her.

"Besides," he went on, warming to his subject, "they're such babies still, so innocent . . . What can they possibly have understood? It was all very artistic. They were only playing dress-up against a white, no-seam backdrop. They'll never know. And, Maddie, there's great money in this stuff . . . great demand."

She felt an emotion of such volcanic force, it resembled nothing she had ever known . . . except, perhaps, the last convulsive push of childbirth.

And with the same kind of low, guttural groan, she grabbed the nearest object at hand and threw it at him as hard as she could.

As luck would have it, that had been the green travertine obelisk bearing the name RAFFERTY PHOTOGRAPHY on all four sides in thirty-six-point Times Roman type. His goddamn logo. She could still hear the strange sound of it striking his head.

Though she felt nothing, not even fear, she thought she might have killed him. She combed through the disorderly studio, throwing the negatives and prints down the incinerator as she found them. Only when she was satisfied that every last vestige of the photo session had been destroyed

24

did she pause to examine the prone figure on the floor. He was alive. She made no effort to determine the seriousness of his injury.

She left the studio.

God, don't let him find us! Please keep him away from us.

She washed her tears away, and then hesitated on the porch a moment before rejoining the girls, trying to present a calm and untroubled face. They were putting wickets up every which way in the field. Perfectly happy and safe.

"Mom, come see! We're setting up the wickets!"

She let them enjoy their game a little while longer. It did her good to watch. Then she rounded them up into the car for their first trip into the village.

The road to town flowed gradually downhill through a stately colonnade of pine trees. The wide-open car windows bathed them in an exhilarating piny warmth. So soothing! So healing! Thank God they'd come here.

"Oh, for heaven's sake. I just realized something. I didn't pay that nice Mr. Mitford our rent! No wonder he seemed to hang about so. He was probably too shy to come right out and ask. I'll just stop by there first."

They rounded a winding curve and there was Indian Meadow: one wide main street with a few cars and pickups parked head-on at an angle on both sides. The street dead-ended into a park and public beach, still closed, on the shores of Blue Mirror Lake, which could be seen to shimmer bluely, as advertised, in the sunlight. The street was called "The Promenade," recalling more fashionable times.

Telling the girls she'd only be a few minutes, Madeleine headed straight for Lakeshore Realty, a large white clapboard building on the corner, full of cupolas, balustrades, and other such high Victorian signatures of the carpenter's art. Its shiny green trim showed signs of a recent repainting.

She entered the shop, and at first it appeared nobody was there. All she heard was the ticking of the old Regulator clock on the wall. Then, as her eyes adjusted to the gloom,

25

she saw a person hunched over a desk in the far corner. Madeleine cleared her throat politely.

"Oh! So sorry. I didn't hear you come in." The startled birdlike woman stood and came swiftly to the front of the shop. "I'm Missie Rollins," she announced brightly. "How may I help you?"

"I was looking for Joe Mitford."

"He isn't in at present. Perhaps *I* can assist you?"

"Well, my name is Madeleine Rafferty, and I've just rented the Perry house."

"Oh! Yes, of course. Did you get your message?"

"Yes, thanks very much. Joe dropped that off for me this morning."

"Good." Missie Rollins adjusted the cuffs of her crisp pale-blue oxford-cloth shirt, which she wore with a stiff plaid skirt that might have been the uniform of some parochial school, and carefully smoothed the pale frizzy blond bun at the very top of her head. Then she removed her reading glasses, allowing them to dangle around her neck from their little beaded chain.

"I'm here now because I made all the arrangements by phone to lease the house and haven't paid the rent yet."

"Oh. Yes. Well, let me see, I certainly should be able to take care of that." She got up and walked to some filing cabinets at the rear. Now Madeleine heard the sound of high-heeled feet approaching heavily from a back room.

"So . . . you're our famous Mrs. Rafferty!" Voice and person made a simultaneous appearance. Both powerful. "How very nice to make your acquaintance. I'm Pamela Perry Mitford. It's such a pleasure to welcome you to Indian Meadow!" She grasped Madeleine's hand in both her own for protracted and ceremonial shaking.

Mrs. Mitford was a tall, stately woman with large hazel eyes and long, prominent teeth. She was dressed in a tweed suit. Her silk blouse was tied into a voluminous bow at the base of her crepey neck and she wore quite a lot of gold jewelry.

26

"Imagine! My son arranged all the details of your rental without even bothering to check with me first! You see, that property is at the present in dispute as part of a divorce proceeding. Mind you, I have always maintained that it's better to have tenants than to leave a place vacant and vulnerable to vandalism and what-all. Good tenants, that is. You being a writer and all from New York, I really can't imagine how the Littlefields could object. . . ."

"Well, that is a surprise. Joe didn't mention there were any problems. He left a nice packet of information for us and all the keys. Actually, I only stopped by just now to pay the first month's rent." Madeleine calculated—correctly, as it turned out—that this might be a good time to put her money where her mouth was and leave this august personage, this imposing matriarch, to handle the litigious Littlefields.

She handed the check—as advanced to her by Matt Blaustein two days earlier—to Mrs. Mitford, who looked at it with respect, and then handed it to Missie.

"Here, Missie, please deposit this into the Littlefield account right away, before the bank closes." Missie grabbed her purse, took the check from Mrs. Mitford, and hurried toward the door. "And, Missie, do watch out with that— that's eight hundred dollars—in case you didn't notice!" Mrs. Mitford cast a stagy look of exasperation Madeleine's way and commented, in a "good help is so hard to find these days" kind of voice, "Sometimes, I don't know *where* her head is at! Now, don't you trouble yourself over any of these, um, loose ends, Mrs., er, Rafferty. We'll take care of everything." Smiling, her teeth and jewelry twinkling brightly, Mrs. Mitford ushered Madeleine to the door.

With a little "Whew!" Madeleine stepped back into the street, spotting the girls over by a park bench. When she caught up to them, she said, "So . . . girls, what do you think? Is this going to be an okay place to live, or what?" She knew they loved it—it stuck out all over them.

They ambled cheerfully down the street until they came

27

to the Blue Mirror Café, which had a telephone sign posted outside. Madeleine ordered two double pistachio ice cream cones for the girls, sat them down in one of the vinyl booths, and went to phone. She'd come prepared with her telephone credit card and Matt Blaustein's home number. The office was closed today—the Friday before Memorial Day.

After three rings, Matt's no-nonsense "Yeah?" greeted her, sounding so familiar and yet so far away. She was stung by homesickness.

"Hello, Matt, this is Madeleine checking in."

"Maddie! Great! I was hoping we'd hear from you today. So, how many chapters have you done so far?"

Madeleine laughed. "Right, Matt. Very funny. Actually, I thought maybe I'd get started on Monday—once we're settled in and everything. Matt, the house is *out of this world*! And there's so much room! You and Sylvie have got to visit us, I know you'd love it."

"No kidding? Say, maybe we will." He paused, and Maddie could picture him studying a wall calendar by the phone, his glasses sliding down his nose, as always. She also heard Sylvie in the background, wanting to know who it was, how she was, *where*?! . . . in the *Adirondacks*? "When?"

"How about some time in July?" she heard Sylvie suggest.

"How about some time in July?" Matt repeated.

"That'd be great! We'd love to have you!"

Then in a different, more subdued tone, Matt asked, "Did you get my message?"

"Yeah. What did he want, did he say?"

"He was, uh, extremely perturbed, Maddie. He seemed real agitated when I told him you didn't work at Dexter anymore. And when I told him you'd left town, I thought he'd have a coronary.

"He said you'd become violent. He had, I dunno, like this butterfly bandage over one eye? And he looked like

28

the wrath of God, so help me, Maddie. He said you weren't, and I quote, *fit* to take the children. It was bad, you know? I had the door closed, but I'm sure it's all over the office. He was drunk or on something, that was obvious.

"But when I told him flat-out that I didn't know *where* you were, that seemed to take the wind out of his sails. He hadn't figured on my saying that. He just accepted it. Maddie, don't you even plan on telling him where you *are*?"

"Matt, *thank you*! Thank you for not telling him. Believe me, the best thing I can do right now is just to keep him away from me and the kids. I wish you didn't have to see him like that, but that's the real Gil Rafferty these days. The other one's long gone." Madeleine's voice was starting to choke up, so Matt broke in.

"Hey, it's cool, kid. You know you can count on me. Don't think about it any more than you can help. Put all your energies into that novel. The old Dexter meter is ticking away, you know, and you're gonna hafta deliver!"

"Right, Matt. And, thanks. You're a real friend."

"So, look . . . better report in to us about once a week, okay? And let me have your number once you get a phone."

"Will do. And, Matt, in spite of everything, I'm really kind of excited to be up here. To be doing this thing. It's an adventure! A whole new life! I really think we're gonna love it here."

"That's the spirit! Speak to you soon. Bye."

"So long. Say hi to Sylvie. Bye."

The second Matt hung up the phone, Sylvie asked, "So . . . how did she sound to you?"

"Okay, actually."

"You didn't tell me she was going all the way up to the *Adirondacks*."

"Don't you go repeating that information to anyone!"

Sylvie looked offended. "Matthew Blaustein . . . are you

suggesting that I don't know when to keep my mouth shut?"

Matt, contrite, walked over to his dear wife of twenty-two years and put his arms around her. "It's just that this is pretty heavy-duty stuff. This Rafferty fellow is a total no-good. And Maddie . . . well, she's been carrying them all for so long . . . I just don't know. What if I made a mistake? What if she breaks down up there? How'm I gonna explain that whopping advance to Mr. Dexter and the board?"

"Matt, it'll work out, you'll see. Trust your instincts."

"That's just it, Sylvie. That's just what's bothering me. This time, I'm afraid I ignored my instincts and let my feelings take over."

"Uh-oh! Now we're really in for it." Sylvie gave him one of her characteristic ironic grins. As far as she was concerned, Matt's instincts and his feelings had always been one and the same . . . and one hundred percent on target.

They crossed the wide expanse of the Promenade to shop at the IGA. Libby and Tillie found this new, country-size store such a novelty that they actually took an interest, helping Madeleine load the little cart with all of their favorite foods. Everything they did up here had an air of playing house to it.

And when at last their laden car again approached the Perry house, it felt—it felt like *home*. Bathed by the golden afternoon sun in sharp relief against the deep-blue sky, it looked like a picture from a child's storybook.

After dinner, Madeleine sat down on one of the big Adirondack chairs out on the porch and watched the girls play a game that entailed the gathering of great quantities of little green berries from a row of bushes by the side of the house. Evidently they were pioneers, eking out a living from the land. The shadows lengthened, the sky stood momentarily suspended in a yellow-greenish half light. The birds began to quiet down for the night. And soon, the two little girls ran up to Maddie, without even being asked, to announce they were ready for bed.

With the setting of the sun, the temperature took a sudden plunge. They went around the house shutting all the windows against the cold mountain air, giggling at their goose bumps and chattering teeth. Out came flannel nighties from the dresser drawer and woolly extra blankets from the big linen closet that smelled faintly of camphor. Libby and Tillie took a hot bath together, which steamed up the window and made the house seem even cozier. Then Madeleine walked up their private stairway with them and made sure they were warmly and happily tucked in for the night.

And then she was alone.

For an instant, she felt a kind of panic. Now what? It was barely past eight o'clock, and all around her was darkness and silence. She was cut off from everything! She wavered on the brink of depression, then pulled back just in time. Sure, she was cut off—but wasn't it wonderful? So pristine! So quiet! Why, this was pure *bliss*.

She reached for a jacket that hung on a hook by the back door and stepped out onto the cold mountainside. The moon was not visible, nor were the stars. There had been a rapid change in the weather, all right; typical, she would soon discover, of this whole region. A drizzling mist had begun, and it smelled wonderful. The deep-woods smell of pine and moss and lake water mingled with the tingly, moisture-laden air and revived Madeleine's spirits like a plunge into a pool. She loved it here! She loved being alone! This was how she would write her book. In this deep quiet, amid this electrifying sense of isolation and closeness to the elements, she would find a story to tell, and the words to tell it with.

She went back inside, latched the door, and walked through the house turning off lights. Then, dressed in a warm flannel robe with an extra shawl wrapped around her shoulders, she sat down at her writing table and considered the shiny package of legal pads. She knew that no matter how formulaic her novel had to be, she wouldn't be able to come up with something she didn't honestly care about. Though she might scoff at the trappings of the romance genre, she wouldn't be able to write with a patronizing, tongue-in-cheek attitude.

The woman I write about will have to be sort of like me, she realized. Someone who's got herself into a jam, but has enough guts to get herself out of it. Someone who runs away from something. A runaway.

She sat there for quite some time . . . before, almost without realizing it, she had opened her package of legal pads, picked up a pen, and begun to write. The small scratching sound of her pen was infinitely soothing, encouraging her to continue on and on.

Part of her could see herself sitting there in the quiet. A woman at a table, writing. Part of her could sense that she was seeing the emergence of a new Madeleine. A Madeleine who might never have been found at all, but for the ordeal of leaving the old one behind.

And perhaps this eerie sense of herself had been induced, in some measure at least, by other eyes that were then focused intently upon the house, from little more than fifty yards away. Eyes that bitterly begrudged the brightly lit bedroom window, shining like a golden paper lantern in the cold dark night.

CHAPTER

4

MADELEINE bounded out of bed the next morning, with a kind of startled energy. Though her body still ached from the hours she'd spent sitting at her desk the night before, she was nonetheless drawn right back to it like a magnet. The sight of the heft of her manuscript folder—nearly twenty pages of notes!—made her proud.

She stood there barefoot in the sharply slanting blue morning shadows, rereading character sketches, scenes, and snippets of dialogue as she began to dress herself.

At first, she'd been quite surprised to find that she was writing a historical novel. Maybe it was living in this old house . . . and that remark of Joe Mitford's about its once having been a station on the Underground Railway.

Yet now, here were these characters, as real to her as any people she might meet in real life, caught up in a small violent current within the larger conflict erupting all around them. A youthful Quaker bride, now a widow and a fugitive as the result of a single bloody incident on the Underground Railway.

From out of nowhere, it seemed, had come a monstrous degenerate of a villain, a poor young girl whose destiny would tie itself up with the Quaker heroine, a hero who seemed quite promising . . . even an orphaned slave baby!

She could *see* it all happening so clearly while she wrote! It was as if she were merely recording events she'd been a witness to.

She stretched, yawned deeply, and then put both hands into the back pockets of her jeans, only to find the check she'd been given by the guy from Mamaroneck, folded into thirds. Over a thousand dollars, and it had completely slipped her mind! She unfolded it and placed it carefully in her "to do" folder. This thin folder, together with her somewhat fatter manuscript folder, now encompassed all the concerns of her new life. A curiously comforting thought.

Now fully dressed except for shoes, Madeleine stepped lazily out onto the porch. The sun had begun to dissipate the heavy dew, and the gray-painted floor boards felt pleasingly warm to the soles of her feet. She took in a deep, luxuriant draft of the mountain air, exhaling with theatrical gusto—"Ahh!"—and began to walk around the property.

She ambled off in the general direction of the toy barn, first passing a clump of small sheds, and then pausing to examine the rough outlines of a former wagon road. Once, back when all this had been a working farm, this would have connected the barn to the main road. She could imagine the big unwieldly wagons, creaking under the weight of their load, pulled by a pair of snorting horses. She thought about her character Phoebe, the Quaker bride, riding west in just such a wagon. How slow it would be . . . how difficult.

And then there was—almost before she could quite register it—a fleeting sensation of something moving. Had she seen something? An animal? She turned back, her stride losing some of its buoyancy. And she felt hungry. In fact, she was ravenous. Well, of course, that's all it was! Laughing at herself for being spooked so easily, she walked to the kitchen door and let herself in. The strange, fleeting sense of vulnerability recurred as she did this, but she could not think why.

It wasn't like Libby and Tillie to sleep so late. She went up the back stairs quietly, not wanting to wake them, really, just wanting to make sure they were all right. And there was Libby sitting bolt upright in her bed, wide awake, the red-framed glasses already firmly in place.

Libby whispered to her, gesturing toward Tillie's bed.

"She was crying real hard . . . but now she's gone back to sleep." Madeleine rushed into the room and sat down on Libby's bed. Poor Libby . . . so serious and responsible. Old enough to catch on to things. Not nearly old enough to be asked to deal with them.

"Why didn't you come get me?"

"Tillie wouldn't *let* me."

"What was the matter?"

In reply, Libby pointed to the stairs, gesturing that they should go down them.

Once they were in the kitchen, Madeleine said, "Now, I want you to tell me exactly what happened."

Libby began to speak, and then seemed to think better of it. Most unlike her. She tried again.

"Mom, you're not going to believe this."

"Try me."

"Okay." Yet there was still quite a pause after that. Finally Libby just blurted, "A ghost."

"A *what*?"

"See. I told you. I knew you'd get like that."

"I'm not being any way. Just tell me. *What?*"

"Last night Tillie went downstairs to go to the bathroom. She saw something at the foot of the stairs. It was all gray, she said, and when it saw her it ran out the back door. She got so scared, she didn't go to the bathroom. She came running upstairs instead and went back to bed. She tried to stay quiet, but then she wet the bed and that made her cry.

35

That woke me up. I wanted to go down and get you, but she wouldn't let me leave her up there all alone. Also, I think she was afraid you'd be mad at her because she wet the bed. But mostly, she didn't want me to leave her alone, and no way was she gonna come back down here, even if I went with her."

"Did *you* see anything or hear anything?"

"I looked out the window, but it was too dark to see anything. But I think I heard something, Ma, like a crunching, like somebody walking or running maybe. It was *really* scary! I almost wet the bed myself."

While Libby talked, Madeleine remembered letting herself in the back door after her morning walk a few minutes ago. She'd locked it the night before. Somebody must have opened that door during the night. She did not say anything about this to Libby.

Instead, she said, "Libby, if there was somebody in this house during the night, you can be sure I'll find out about it . . . and you can also be very sure that it wasn't a ghost. Tell you what. Let's look around and see if we can find any clues, okay?" She stood up, reaching for Libby's hand. Libby shrank back.

"Uh, I dunno, Ma, what if there's still ghosts around?"

"Hey, I've been up for hours. I've walked all around the place, and I haven't seen anything unusual"—to speak of. She added the last part silently to herself.

They went to the back door. There were some footprints—dewy grit and pine needles from outside—but those could have been her own. She closed the back door again with a little slam. That caused the door of the linen closet to swing open with a creaky noise, and they both jumped. Another door Madeleine could remember closing firmly last night after they'd helped themselves to extra blankets.

Madeleine walked to the closet and opened the door all the way. Libby's eyes were fairly popping with fear.

Madeleine peered inside. "Come see for yourself, Libby.

36

There are no ghosts here. Just the sheets and towels and blankets that have been here all along."

But even as she said this, she noticed that the bottom shelf showed obvious signs of disarray. It had contained three orderly stacks of blankets: khaki, navy blue, and gray. But now the gray stack was shorter, mussed up, toppled down. Had their "gray ghost" been an intruder who'd taken that missing gray blanket and wrapped up in it to ward off the cold?

"You know, Libby, maybe some stranger got very cold last night. So terribly cold that he came in here to get warm. We'll probably never see him or her again."

Libby said thoughtfully, "You mean somebody was out there freezing last night, like a bag lady? Do they have them up here, too?"

"I don't know, honey. But if the person had meant to do us any harm, would he or she have run away from a little five-year-old girl? Of course not. No, I'll bet it was just some poor person down on their luck, trying to find a way to keep warm. Sad, isn't it?" She put her arms around Libby, and they returned to the kitchen for breakfast.

The explanation seemed to satisfy Libby. But Madeleine found the idea of an actual intruder violating their mountain fastness had stirred up all sorts of fears. She knew beyond all doubt that she had locked both doors, front and back, from the inside, the night before. Yet the rear door had opened when she'd come in from her early-morning walk. How had he/she/it managed to get in? Was it someone with a key? It had to have been.

How much did she really know about this place? Or the estranged couple who owned it? And those weird Mitfords. What about them? Were they on the level? She had foolishly let herself believe she'd stumbled onto an island of peace and tranquillilty in an otherwise hostile world. But this was also the world. And she knew nobody here . . . nobody at all.

She looked back on their visit to Indian Meadow the day

before, and suddenly it seemed to her that the villagers had been sullen and unresponsive. Wasn't it always open season on "summer people"? Madeleine's instincts were telling her she ought not to be in too big a hurry to report the intruder. With no other adult around to corroborate it, her story might be dismissed as the hysterical imaginings of a spoiled city woman . . . and newly single mother, at that. There was a lot more at stake here for them than just two weeks in the mountains. She'd best go easy.

Madeleine went upstairs to deal with Tillie and found her half-awake and more than ready for the loving attention she duly received.

"It's scary here at night, Mommy," Tillie confided. "It's so quiet. There's nobody else around. Sometimes I think the house is gonna fall right off the mountain! I wake up just to make sure it's still standing where it was when I went to sleep."

"You poor baby—why didn't you tell me?"

"Oh, when morning comes, I sort of forget about it. But when I saw that ghost lady last night . . . I was afraid she'd come after me. She didn't, though. She ran away."

"The *lady*? You think it was a lady?"

"Yeah, I guess." Tillie didn't realize she'd provided new information.

"I'm sorry I wet the bed. I didn't mean to! It was an accident!" She was beginning to cry again.

"Never mind, honey. It's all right, really. Come, you can help me wash out the sheets in the laundry shed."

According to Mitford's instructions, the gray-shingled outbuilding that served as the laundry shed contained a functioning washer and dryer. The key turned easily in the padlock. Except for a few oddments left about on shelves— an old half-empty box of laundry detergent, some clothes-line and clothespins, a bag of old forgotten clothes—the room was clean and bare. She opened the lid to the washer, dropped in the sheets, turned the knob, and was instantly rewarded by the sound of gushing water. The machine was apparently in perfect working order.

They sat lazily on the front stoop of the shed, listening to the machine churning, content that something useful was being accomplished.

Gazing up at the limitless blue sky gave Madeleine the idea to put up a clothesline. She got the girls to help her string the rope around the trunks of two trees, and then found they still had enough left over to bring back to the wall of the shed, where an obliging nail helped them complete the *L*-shaped arrangement. Neither Libby nor Tillie had ever hung wash outside to dry before. Tillie had never even seen a clothespin! Madeleine had to demonstrate how it worked. Tillie was impressed.

"This is a good idea, Mom!" she said, as though Madeleine had just invented it. They found a box for Tillie to stand on while they draped the sheets over the line. It was her job to fasten the pins at regular intervals.

Tillie stepped back and admired her accomplishment, satisfaction exuding from her entire being. Libby and Madeleine exchanged a look—like indulgent parents—acknowledging that the five-year-old had obviously recovered from her earlier fright. Then the girls began to dart crazily in and out between the sheets, giggling, playing some game.

Leaving the wash to dry, Madeleine and the girls drove into the village. To their surprise, they found the Promenade strung with red, white, and blue banners in honor of Memorial Day. A band was just lining up, preparing to march down the street. They parked the car hurriedly and rushed to a curbside spot to watch. A reviewing stand heaped in patriotic bunting had been erected at the entrance to Blue Mirror Lake. Apparently Memorial Day weekend was a very important holiday here in Indian Meadow, not only as an occasion to honor its valiant war dead but, perhaps more important, as the kick-off for its major peacetime livelihood: the summer tourist season.

A whistle blew, and the band, braving the hot midday sun in heavy green flannel blazers and cream-colored gabardine pants, snapped smartly to attention. "The Stars and Stripes Forever" struck up, and off they marched, almost in unison. Two trumpets, a saxophone, a clarinet, a flute, a piccolo, a couple of drums, and a magnificent tuba—played by an altogether amiable and willing confluence of disparate social and musical backgrounds.

Observing the villagers in this setting, Madeleine found it hard to hold on to her earlier stereotype of dour, suspicious backwoods types. Those brooding undercurrents she'd imagined up there on her isolated mountainside now seemed foolishly melodramatic.

Madeleine had just recognized Missie Rollins laboring studiously on the clarinet when she felt a tap on her shoulder. She jumped. It was that kind of tap.

"Isn't this a wonderful day for our parade?" Mrs. Mitford, wearing a masterly assemblage of red, white, and blue garments, greeted her like a fond friend.

"Wonderful," Madeleine agreed.

"Oh! And these must be your two little girls. Joseph mentioned them to me. Oh, my, aren't they precious?" Madeleine looked over Mrs. Mitford's commanding shoulder to see the somewhat sheepish figure of Joe standing by.

"Hello, Joe! Nice to see you again. We're so glad we happened to be in town to see this."

"Well, now. It's a fine parade. We have it every year, you know. That's, uh, our Missie over there playing the clarinet—" One eye seemed to follow Missie Rollins as she slowly marched down the street, while the other had fixed itself on Madeleine at the curbside.

"Oh, and by the way, Mrs. Rafferty," Mrs. Mitford interrupted, "I hope you didn't worry about the possibility of any, er, irregularities with your stay at the Perry house. We will see to everything, I assure you."

"I never gave it another thought, Mrs. Mitford. I'm glad we caught this parade. It's a very nice band."

The Mitfords waved and moved on, stopping to chat with other citizens in a cordial, ceremonial manner. Madeleine realized they were on their way to take seats of honor on the speaker's platform.

One of the speakers was an earnest young spokesman for the Adirondack Council with an alarming update on the fight to save the Adirondack Park, which had reached a critical stage. In the last year alone, thousands of undeveloped acres of wild forested land that should have been preserved through public acquisition had been lost to subdividers. Bureaucratic stumbling blocks had kept the Department of Environmental Conservation from acquiring these large private holdings as they became available. Ironically, it wasn't for lack of money that EnCon had lost these acquisitions; a $250 million bond act had been allocated specifically for that purpose. Yet not one dollar had so far been spent for Adirondack land. While EnCon faltered over such matters as easement, appraisal, and accessibility, private developers moved in. What was lost to the state would be lost forever. What they saved, they would save for good.

And then, a bustling annual fair opened Blue Mirror Lake Park officially for the season.

By the time they returned to the Perry house again, it was nearly eight o'clock. They'd sampled so much delicious food at the various booths, that there was no need to make dinner. Though both girls definitely needed a bath.

"Why don't we run the tub, and you guys can play with your new Indian canoes. Then I'll go take the sheets down from the line, okay?"

"Okay!" They ran to their bag of goodies and retrieved their authentic, plastic, Made-in-Taiwan replicas of birchbark canoes. Madeleine filled the tub, and they settled in.

"I'll be right back, kids—just want to take those sheets down before it gets dark."

"Uh-huh." They didn't look up from their task at hand, which evidently was to fill up their canoes with soap suds.

She opened the back door. The sun was going down and there was a chill wind. She reached for the red-and-black-checked jacket that hung by the door and walked out.

The wind rushing up the mountainside almost took her breath away. Deep pewter-colored clouds tinged with dark coral from the sun's imminent departure scudded rapidly across the sky. She rounded the path to the laundry shed and was pleased to see the sheets had stayed on the line.

It still amazed her to see how rapidly night came on here on the mountain. The gathering dark was almost complete. In their shrill white contrast, the crisp stirring sheets seemed to give off a light of their own, a kind of phosphorescence.

She drew nearer to the clothesline and heard a sound that was distinctly out of harmony with the chorus of natural night noises all around her. She stopped to listen, hesitating, not sure where the sound had come from.

Just then, the sheets began to surge and roil with an uncanny force. In a kind of frenzied animation, they suddenly swept directly toward her.

She was encircled. With a muffled scream, Madeleine fought to disentangle herself—until her arms were yanked back and twisted painfully behind her. She was trapped.

A brutal, viselike grip held her totally immobilized.

CHAPTER

5

"*DAMN you! Where in hell have you been?*"

It was a low, resonant voice Madeleine had never heard before. Not Gil's. Even as she feared that it might be Gil, her body sensed it was not. Who, then? A rapist? A local crazy? The ghost?

And then the viselike hold loosened, the shroud of sheeting came undone, and she found herself looking into the shadowy face of a dark-eyed man she'd never seen before.

"Who are you?" He dropped his hold on her, stepping back, his hands raised in a palms-out parody of dismay, as though she might be radioactive or something. "I . . . I thought you were my wife. . . ." Naturally, that explained everything, including the utter brutality of the hold.

"That's funny," Madeleine managed to reply, though her voice shook, "for a second there, I thought *you* might be my husband."

She was so relieved to be alive and returned to the world of civil discourse that she just stood there rubbing her wrists, which hurt, and waited for whatever else he had to say for himself.

"Uh, my wife's pulled this disappearing act, you see. I was so sure you were . . . that jacket . . . it's just like the one she wears when she's up here. . . ." He drifted off. The enormity of his error was beginning to sink in. "Who *are* you? What on earth brings you here?"

"I'm Madeleine Rafferty and I *live* here. I've rented the Perry house."

"You've *what*? Rented? From *whom*? I *own* the damn place, and I don't know anything about it!"

"The Mitfords leased it to me."

"Shit. I've been away. I didn't know. I thought Joe had hired a caretaker. How long are you here for, then?"

"Six months."

"Six *months*! Jesus Christ! They really should have checked with me first, wouldn't you think? Ah, hell, look, I'm sorry about all this." He waved his hand in the direction of the sheets, now hanging limply and barely visible in the black night. "My name is Harry Littlefield." He offered his hand.

Madeleine decided it was too dark to see it.

"Mr. Littlefield, I've got to get back to the house. I left my two daughters in the bath." She plucked the sheets from the line and blundered down the pitch-dark path to the house. She assumed he would follow but didn't particularly care either way. She was angry. The house glowed with light and warmth, but it seemed distant and difficult to reach.

She opened the back door and realized she hadn't been gone more than a couple of minutes. The girls were playing the same game, were talking in the same nonsensical singsong way, filling their new toy canoes with sudsy water and pouring it out again. She began to fold Tillie's sheets.

Littlefield appeared in the doorway. He hesitated, waiting to be invited in. Madeleine saw no way out of it.

"Girls," she said, "we have a visitor."

Libby, who was seated at the far end of the tub, could see just enough of the back entrance to realize that the visitor was a man. Outraged, she grabbed a washcloth, held it up to her flat little chest, and screamed.

"Argh! A man! Get him out of here! We're naked!"

It was all Madeleine could do not to laugh.

"It's okay, Libby, we're going to the other room." She ushered Mr. Littlefield into the living room.

"A fine set of lungs on her," Littlefield remarked.

"That sense of drama comes from years of too much television," Madeleine said dryly. "Luckily she's found so many better things to do since we've come here."

"I guess you like it here, then."

"Very much."

"Look. You've got nothing to worry about, Mrs., um, Rafferty. I'm not about to give you a hard time. I can't begin to apologize for my behavior out there. I've been trying to locate my wife for weeks, now. I thought maybe she might have come up here . . . although to tell you the truth, it did seem like the last place she'd have come to. She hated it here. In fact, I guess you could say this house is where our marriage really fell apart. Still, I'd run out of places to look—"

Madeleine interrupted him. "Mr. Littlefield, I have problems of my own. I'm sorry for your trouble, but frankly, I don't see that it's any business of mine. I'm sure if you just talk to the Mitfords, they'll explain the arrangements I've made and that you'll find everything quite satisfactory."

"Of course. I'm sure everything will be, uh, perfectly satisfactory." He was stung by her rudeness and she was glad. "I'll be staying in town for a few days, I guess, in case . . . that is, if you should hear anything . . . oh, never mind. Good-bye."

He went out the front door, almost slamming it. Madeleine was agitated. She heard the engine on his car start and wished she hadn't handled the scene so badly. But

45

how was she supposed to react to such a brutal and terrifying experience?

By the time she got the girls off to bed, she'd almost succeeded in shaking off the effect of Mr. Littlefield's attack. She did wonder, for a moment, whether perhaps she ought to have mentioned their nighttime visitor to him. But what would that have accomplished? The very idea of his hanging around, searching the premises for a vanished intruder, made her shudder.

Once the children were asleep, the house quieted down to the mountain hush she loved so much. Again, she locked both the front door and the back door, pausing first to step out for a breath of the night air, for one more glimpse of the clear starry sky and the sharp slope of land resting darkly beneath it.

And again, she was observed.

And then, surprisingly, their first week on the mountain, begun in such intense agitation, began to smooth out. The days began to take on a languorous, luxuriant anonymity.

"Is this Tuesday?"

"No, that was yesterday."

"No, by golly, that was the day *before* yesterday. Remember? That was when the guy came from the phone company."

The new phone, installed in the kitchen, had been used just once: to inform Matt Blaustein of their number.

Most mornings, Madeleine would type up what she'd written out in longhand the night before. She had rigged up a worktable out on the front porch, plugging her typewriter into an extension cord that was strung through the living room window and inserted into a wall outlet. She'd actually begun the manuscript, and Chapter One was making respectable headway.

On Friday, they woke to find their mountain transformed by a heavy canopy of jungle damp. No air stirred, and the sky shimmered sickly white. They abandoned the Perry house for the fabled attractions of Blue Mirror Lake. The calm water—brownish yellow when you actually stepped into it—was cool and welcoming.

As the day progressed, the threatening damp tightened its grip. The sky seemed to absorb more and more moisture, refusing to release a single drop. Above the gentle lapping sounds of the lake, buzzing insects sounded raspy, mechanical. Few birds were inspired to sing.

Then, from some ridge to the west of them, they began to discern a distant rumble. Tillie's eyes lit up.

"Thunder!"

"Yeah!"

"Okay, girls, just a few more minutes in the water. We want to be home before that gets here."

They stopped in town for groceries. Madeleine wheeled her cart through the narrow aisles of the IGA and suddenly remembered Mr. Littlefield. He'd said he would be staying in town for a few days. She hoped they wouldn't see him. Come to think of it, she wasn't sure she'd recognize him. She had a problem remembering faces to begin with, and she'd been so upset when they met, she had barely looked at him. She seemed to remember his eyes. Though what it was about them exactly that she remembered, she couldn't say.

She did remember to buy candles and was rather proud of herself for that. Up here in the mountains, storms like the one that seemed to be approaching often caused power failures. It was good to be prepared for the worst.

Anxious to beat the storm, they hurried back up the mountain.

They might as well have taken their time.

If anything, the sultriness merely increased. Madeleine threw together a large salad, and they sat out under a tree to eat it.

"When's it gonna rain?" Tillie complained, fanning her shirt out from a newly muscular middle.

Now and then the sky would shudder with a sulfurous

flash of yellow, answered in time by a teasing murmur from someplace far away.

It would surely rain. But not soon. Madeleine regretted abandoning the lake in such a dumb hurry.

"I know what let's do!" Libby said. "Let's play in the toy barn!"

"Good idea! I'll just go in and get the key and meet you there." They were off and running before she'd finished the sentence.

In the barn, the thick stone foundation and ancient earthen floor created a cool, timeless climate all its own. Small windows under the eaves admitted sharply slanting columns of daylight, making artificial illumination unnecessary. In response to the cathedral-like hush of the place, the girls spoke almost in whispers. They searched the lower shelves and found an old Go to the Head of the Class board game, which they fell to playing with absolute absorption.

Madeleine sat down in a lovely blue-green Windsor chair around the corner, within easy earshot, and closed her eyes.

She began to inhabit the world of her story and soon lost all sense of time and place. So much so, that the distant retorts of the hesitating storm became nineteenth-century gunshots. Suddenly and with such vivid force, it made her teeth clench; there was danger in the air. She watched, helplessly, as Lena, an important character in her book, a willful, capricious girl whom Madeleine had assumed would be around until the conclusion, was shot and fell.

Having "seen" it, did she have to put it down that way? Couldn't she spare this girl who, for all her faults, enlivened every scene she'd been a part of? The shooting had played so clearly before her, it was etched in her mind now. No going back. She was gone. The gunshots faded.

At last the Adirondack thunder grew closer. In response, Madeleine's story conjured up a stormy image. It was night and Phoebe, the lone survivor, frightened and defenseless, drenched to the skin by a downpour, was illuminated by a brilliant flash of lightning that was so close, there was an actual smell of—

"*Mom!*"

Tillie and Libby were vying for lap room. That had been very, very close! She could smell the gunpowdery smell of lightning in the air. Another bolt. A deafening crash.

"*Oh!*"

"*Oh!*"

"*Oh!*"

They huddled together, waiting it out.

"You know, girls," Madeleine said during a brief lull, "this old barn's lived through a lot of storms in its day. I'm sure we're just as safe as—" Only to be interrupted by a galvanic crack intent upon challenging her presumption.

Now huge drops could be heard to spatter, gathering force, fusing into a roar, drowning out all possibility of further talk among them. And still the thunder boomed and the vicious bolts of lightning crackled. The barn, once such a massive fortress, creaked and groaned piteously.

Tillie began to cry.

This storm seemed not about to stop any time soon. If they were going to get back to the house at all, they'd simply have to make a dash for it.

It had become too dark to see anything. She could barely make out the edge of the big door. But that's where the light switch was. With a gesture, she told the girls to stay put and went to try the switch. It worked. No power lines down yet, anyway.

In the vast collection of sports equipment that hung from the rafters, Madeleine hoped to find a tarpaulin or canvas cover of some sort that she could throw around themselves when they ran through the drenching storm. Then she saw something even better slung on a hook high on the side wall: a huge old-fashioned yellow oilskin slicker. By standing on tiptoe and stretching to her very limit, she was able

49

to graze the bottom of it with enough force to send it tumbling down, landing on the earthen floor with a thump.

She hoisted the archaic garment, redolent of fish oil, around her shoulders and encircled Libby and Tillie on either side of her. Arms wound about one another, oilskin flapping like some antique aeroplane straining for liftoff, they lunged up the path in the swooshing, splashing rain. Strobelike flashes of noon-bright lightning right there on the path in front of them created such a clamor of confusion they didn't even hear themselves. They were all three screaming at the top of their lungs.

And then they were home. Safe. Soon they might even be dry again. Certainly they were no longer, any of them, hot.

"Wow! You guys were terrific out there. I'm proud of you."

Armed with fresh towels, Libby and Tillie went up to their room to change.

The storm had slackened by the time they returned to the kitchen dressed in pajamas, though it was only seven in the evening. They were sitting contentedly at the kitchen table and devouring a snack of cereal and bananas when the lights went out.

"It's okay. I remembered to buy candles."

They set the candles about on saucers, and as the number of candles multiplied, the small flickering lights cast a lovely, fragrant spell. For a time, it seemed enough just to sit there and admire the kitchen's transformation by candlelight—until the storm could be heard coming closer yet again. Before they knew it, the raindrops, which had diminished to a soothing patter, became as noisy as kettledrums again and water began pouring past their windows in slick, silver sheets. A booming clap of thunder made the girls shriek and put their hands over their ears.

Tillie was fighting back tears. Libby's jaw was set, her gaze serious and inward. Cuddling both girls on her lap for a few moments, Madeleine pondered the difference between the predictable thundershowers she was familiar with down in the city, which moved from west to east and were over in twenty minutes, and this puzzling Adirondack variety, which moved in circles, diminishing only to return full force just as they'd let their defenses down.

She settled the girls into bed, leaving a candle by their doorway. Despite their anxiety, they would probably sleep well. They'd thoroughly exhausted themselves.

Which left her alone, with anxieties of her own.

She blew out some candles, carried others with her into her bedroom. And then, to her irritation, found the candlelight impossible to read or write by. She put away her manuscript with a sigh. A whole day shot. What if the electricity didn't return tomorrow? How would she type?

She plopped herself down in one of the easy chairs by the window and looked out at the wet black night, which was lit up sporadically to reveal the slope of the front yard, the laundry shed, a corner of the barn's roof.

She'd try to think some more about her story, pick up where she'd left off in the toy barn. Did she really have to let Lena die? That just left Phoebe, who was not nearly as interesting, being rather earnest and strait-laced. Ah, but maybe allowing the reader to witness her gradual transformation into a passionate, aggressive woman. . . . Now, that was more like it! Thinking of Phoebe, Madeleine smiled at her blurry reflection in the rain-streaked window.

Just then, there was an intense crack of thunder and a multiple flash of lightning that illuminated a scene so like the one imagined by Madeleine earlier that day she thought at first it must be illusory, her fevered imagination working overtime. But, no . . . it kept on. Every flash of lightning merely showed the young woman farther advanced in her apparent attempt to run from the laundry shed to the barn.

She was soaked to the skin.

Her dark hair was plastered to her head.

She appeared to be running for her very life.

And she was real. As real as the terror that now propelled her right out of the picture framed by Madeleine's window.

CHAPTER

6

MADELEINE'S first impulse upon seeing the wraithlike girl disappear behind the barn was simply to rush out after her. But halfway out the door—and already soaked—she hesitated. It was pitch dark out there. How could she know where the girl might be hiding—or worse, lurking?

She closed the door and walked through the house to the back door, retrieving the yellow slicker from where it lay in a tentlike heap. She put it on. The floor-length coat made an eerie rattling sound as it hit the backs of her ankles on her way back through the house. Then there she stood again at the opened front door, with nothing to see but shiny blackness and nothing to hear but the rain. Water was streaming thickly from the porch and sweeping down the steps like a cataract in full spate.

In the next flash of lightning, the dark-haired woman was suddenly revealed—full size—standing directly in front of her on the porch.

"You must let me in. I can't take any more."

In her shock, Madeleine found herself focusing on the

prosaic. She put her finger to her lips and replied, "Shh. We mustn't wake my children."

The dark, dripping creature understood. She placed an admonitory finger to her own lips and entered the house on tiptoe, her every step releasing a small silvery splash of water.

Madeleine saw to towels, a robe, slippers . . . and finally the girl sat at the table with a hot cup of tea before her. Madeleine watched her relax at last in the calm candlelit kitchen, sipping tea. Now she would hear her story, and all the mystery would be dispelled. Contrarily, she was almost sorry to let it go.

The stranger was a woman more nearly Madeleine's own age than she had seemed to be at first. Madeleine had already guessed her to be the hotly pursued Mrs. Littlefield and was determined to help her in any way possible.

"My name is Madeleine Rafferty," she said, to start her talking.

"My name is Rose Bedard," the woman replied, hardly giving Madeleine time to abandon her preconception as she launched into a rapid-fire narrative. "Joe Mitford hired me to be a caretaker here at the Perry house and then he turned around and fired me. He paid me the full amount of money anyway, but I had to promise to leave right away. I took the money, but I couldn't leave. That was nearly two weeks ago, and I've been hiding out here ever since. You know, I'm so hungry I could— Do you have anything to go with this tea?"

"I don't understand. Why did he fire you? Was it something you did?" Madeleine took out bread, cheese, eggs, bacon, some leftover macaroni salad, and grapes and began to scramble the eggs. Rose got up, found a frying pan, and put the bacon in.

"It wasn't anything I did, nothing like that. Joe just said that things'd changed and he wouldn't be needing me after all. He said hiring me had been a mistake and his mom was real mad at him. He's like a . . . well, a mama's boy, you know? I think what actually happened is that they'd got this chance for a big commission by renting the place for lots of money."

Madeleine thought of the times since their arrival when she would sense the shadowy brush of something very like hostility coming from somewhere nearby. Rose must have hated them for moving into this wonderful house and dislocating her! Yet here she was now, turning the bacon in the pan, her very pretty face positively beatific at the prospect of a decent meal. No hostility whatsoever.

"But why didn't you just take the money Joe Mitford paid you and leave?"

"And how far would three hundred dollars have taken me, eh? That's all I got. See the reason I took the job was to have a rent-free place."

"But how were you planning to live on a hundred dollars a month?"

"Ah, that was just pocket money, my own to do with as I pleased. I've already spent it a dozen times over in my mind. I get money to live on from my boyfriend. That's why I had to stay here. There's no way to get in touch with him to tell him there's been a change of plans. There's trouble with our families, you know . . . oh, never mind, it's such a long story. Anyway, he'll be coming for me here, and I've got to be here for him. There's just a whole bunch of reasons, you know?"

Madeleine most assuredly did *not* know.

"Where is he now, your boyfriend?"

"His name is Jake, Jake Charpentier, and he's doing construction for some cousins of his up in Canada, building a ski resort, being paid under the table."

"You're both from around here?"

"Oh, yeah. Indian Meadow, Placid, over to Burlington . . . we're all local. My mom used to work right here at the Perry house for Joe Mitford's mom. I guess I've known them all my life. And of course I know this place like the back of my hand. I even had some keys Joe didn't know I had. So I was able to stay in the barn at first, and it really wasn't all that bad. But then one day, out of the blue, the lock on the barn gets changed on me. I had all my stuff stashed in there! I never got any of it back. I've been holed up in that dumb laundry shed ever since."

"How awful!" Madeleine refilled Rose's plate and poured her another cup of tea.

"It gets worse. Today, I went into the woods to pick some greens and maybe catch me a fish in the pond. I've been existing on Slim Jims and peanut butter crackers from the machines down at the gas station. I didn't want to risk being seen in town buying groceries. Anyway, I needed some real food for a change. So there I was in the woods when it began to look like a storm was coming up. I forgot about fishing and headed back. When I passed the barn, I could hardly believe my eyes. The door was wide open!"

"What time was this?" Madeleine thought it was probably when she'd been there with the girls.

"Oh, around three o'clock, I guess."

"No, that wasn't us. We did go there later, though."

"Oh, I know it wasn't you. I *heard* who it was. It was that Mrs. Littlefield—the lady who used to live here?—talking to someone about all those old toys, making them sound like they were these priceless collector's items. Well, I just dashed in quiet as a mouse, picked up my stuff from where I'd hidden it, and hightailed it right out of there. I didn't want anybody seeing me. I don't know who it was she was talking to, it could've been a Mitford—"

Madeleine interrupted. "But you are sure it was Mrs. Littlefield?"

"Oh, yeah, there's no mistaking her—she's got a thick New York accent and a very loud voice. 'Oh, do you really like it? I got it at a little boutique down in SoHo!'"

They both laughed. Rose had a good ear.

"Yes, I do know the type."

"So there I am running to the laundry shed with all my belongings clutched in my arms. I get to the shed, and I can't find the key anywhere! Can you believe that? It must have dropped out of my pocket while I was running. So now I don't even have a place to get in out of the rain! Those were the only keys I had—the key to the toy barn that got changed and the key to the laundry shed that I lost."

Madeleine wasn't so sure she believed that. Couldn't Rose have been the one who helped herself to a desperately needed blanket on that cold night? It certainly made sense. Yes, Rose had probably been their gray ghost. Another mystery explained. But even if it had been her, Madeleine couldn't find it in her heart to blame her. Under similar circumstances, she'd probably have done the same thing. And Madeleine doubted she would want to admit to owning a key to the main house herself.

"I don't like thunder and lightning storms all that much to begin with," Rose went on, "but this one has got to be the worst we've had in years. By the time it actually started to come down, the only cover I could find was under the eaves of the laundry shed. I think I must have stood there for hours. I got so cold and wet and scared, I just couldn't stand it anymore! I started running all over the place. I swear I was almost struck by lightning at one point. I could've dropped dead right there! I kept trying all the doors on the outbuildings hoping to find some place to go to. But every damn door was locked tighter than a drum. Finally, I didn't care about what Joe Mitford would do if he found out I'm still here. I just couldn't take another minute of being outside."

"Rose, Joe Mitford can't do anything to you."

"I took his money and promised to leave."

"Give the money back to him."

"What?"

"I mean, there's no reason why you can't just stay on here with us. Until Jake comes for you, that is. You could help with the kids and the meals and stuff. I'd pay you a hundred dollars a week plus room and board. I could use some help." Madeleine did not know she was going to say any of this until she heard it coming out of her mouth. What was she getting into? And yet, despite the peculiarly chaotic life she'd apparently been leading, Rose had completely won Madeleine over. Or maybe because of it. After all, had Madeleine's life been any less chaotic?

"You're offering me a *job*?"

"Sure. Why not? You know how to take care of kids, don't you?"

"Of course I do. I've got three of my own, don't I?"

"Good grief, Rose, and where are *they*?"

"Oh, not to worry. They're with my folks in Vermont. They love it there. I think that's probably where Joe thought I would go. But like I said earlier, neither Jake's folks nor mine are all that happy about our being together. I didn't want to have to stay with them. Once Jake comes back from Canada, we're buying us a brand-new twenty-four-foot mobile home and going to live like a real family. Our folks will come 'round eventually."

"Okay, then. What do you say?"

"I can't believe you're actually doing this. I'd love to work for you, Mrs. um, Rafferty. I can't wait to see your girls up close. They seem real nice."

So it was decided. Madeleine helped Rose move into one of the upstairs bedrooms, and then, satisfied with a decent day's accomplishment, went straight to bed herself.

The next morning, Libby and Tillie, up early, were dazzled to discover Rose already at work in the kitchen.

"What's your name? Where did you come from? Will you play with us? Come up and see our room! We used to live in New York, but now we live here. Come see our toys!" They darted about her, barely waiting for her replies, grabbing her hand and dragging her upstairs to their room. Despite these gratifying distractions, Rose had breakfast ready and waiting for Madeleine's entrance half an hour later.

"Wow! Good morning, guys. Look at that! I think I can get used to this."

"Hi, Mom! This is Rose. She's from Indian Meadow. She's mostly French-Canadian, but a little bit Indian, too. She's gonna stay here with us. Don't you think she's pretty? She knows how to canoe and she's gonna teach us. She knows how to ride horses and she's gonna teach us."

"And she's gonna take us into Indian Meadow this morning and we're going swimming in the lake. . . ."

"That's *great*! That's *terrific*! Now why don't we all just sit down and have some breakfast, okay?"

By some miraculous sleight-of-hand, Rose organized Libby and Tillie into a smoothly functioning kitchen crew who restored the place to perfect order in a matter of minutes when breakfast was done. Then, as she was rounding them up for the ride into Indian Meadow, she told Madeleine, "I'm going to do like you said and give Joe Mitford back his money."

"Good. You'll see, that'll straighten out the whole mess."

Madeleine stood on the porch watching them drive off. She could hardly believe her good luck. Blissfully unencumbered, she set up her typing table and went straight to work. She wrote until about eleven, when she decided to take a break . . . a short walk.

After last night's raging storm, the morning was as mild as milk. The sunshine seemed bland, diffused by a slight haze. There were still droplets everywhere on the leaves and in the grass, reflecting the light like prisms. Madeleine chose the path that headed toward the pond.

She'd only gone a short way when she caught sight of something moving and stopped. No more than ten feet from where she stood, a glossy-coated doe and two beautiful fawns were now standing stock-still. They began to sniff the wind with round-eyed alertness. Madeleine held her breath and watched as, apparently unaware of her existence, they then moved placidly and gracefully across the

58

clearing. Suddenly, there was a rapidly accelerating sound of muffled hooves as they leaped along the bracken at the edge of the woods and were gone. Elegant cuneiform notations were all that remained to mark their recent diagonal path. And only then did Madeleine remember to exhale.

Somewhat stunned by the beauty of that encounter, she continued on her walk. Her head was down, looking at the muddy path in hopes of spotting more tracks. Instead, she spied a rosy orange salamander walking purposefully in front of her. She kneeled down and picked him up—all two and a half inches of him—to study the beautiful markings along his back. He suffered her attentions patiently enough but seemed to move along rather more urgently once she returned him safely to the ground.

She began to round the pond, heading for the farther shore. Though there was no cleared path, simply using her legs forcefully let her bushwhack through the undergrowth. There had probably been a trail here at one time.

Soon, however, the soggy ground became too mucky for her to continue. Holding on to tree trunks to keep from sliding, she clambered up to higher ground the better to survey the scene below. She could see the small rain-swollen stream that fed the pond rushing rapidly over mossy cobbles, overshooting its banks in spots, nearly stopped in its tracks at one point by an impenetrable bottleneck of fallen logs and crisscrossed branches. A beaver dam? Could be.

She made her way down for a closer look, stepping gingerly from rock to rock, avoiding mud to one side, icy water on the other. Her powers of concentration became fully engaged by the childish fun of maintaining her balance while treading on the slick, unpredictable surfaces.

She had just misjudged the solidity of a flat stone, resulting in one foot's slipping suddenly ankle-deep in muck, and was stepping cautiously onto a thick log, when it rolled right out from under her.

She landed on both knees painfully. Loosened by the impact, a tangled mass of debris close by rose up in the water with a swooshy gurgling sound. Then in a kind of dread slow motion, its incomprehensible component parts began to emerge—one hideous, lifeless, waterlogged gray limb at a time.

Freed of its slippery mooring among branches and twigs, it sought the surface of the water like some ghostly dolphin. And there—face down, bobbing rhythmically—it remained. Madeleine saw the smooth, thin grayish back, the torn shreds of clothing, the tangled mat of black hair . . . and then she could see no more.

Gagging, sobbing, retching, she slogged pell-mell through the shallow water, tripping and falling, mindless of the drenching cold, until somehow she'd reached the dock and was running blindly down the path to the house.

While she ran, the image of what she'd seen refused to fade, continued to play repeatedly in her mind's eye. Details she hadn't absorbed in her shock came unavoidably into focus now. Though the body had been face down, for example, she knew that she had seen the body of a woman. For one moment, the gray swollen hands had seemed to reach out—a swimmer grabbing for the edge of the pool, and missing—and there was bright crimson polish on what must have once been impeccable fingernails.

Soaking wet, her shirt stained with vomit, Madeleine stumbled up the porch steps. She rushed into the house knowing she must phone the police—and stopped, momentarily too distraught to think. Where was the goddamn phone in this house? She couldn't remember! She dashed from her bedroom to the living room, into the kitchen. If only her heart would stop pounding so loud, maybe she could find . . . do . . . what was it? Call. She had to call for help. The phone was in the kitchen. She was in the kitchen. Now all she had to do was—

"Mrs. Rafferty? Are you here? May I come in? It's Harry Littlefield again. Rose told me my wife was here. . . . Hello?"

He stepped into the kitchen and saw Madeleine standing with the telephone receiver in her hand, her face a blank mask of shock.

"Mrs. Rafferty! What is it? What's wrong?"

"Oh, God!" A horrible coughing sob. She collapsed and he caught her in outstretched arms.

"What's happened? Are you hurt?" He held her. She was crying too hard to speak.

Then she looked up at him and said with utter clarity and certainty, "Oh, God, Mr. Littlefield. Your *wife!*"

CHAPTER

7

HARRY Littlefield sat Madeleine down. Carefully, he removed the telephone receiver she still held in her hand and replaced it in its cradle on the wall. This gave him time to prepare himself for what was coming.

"Your wife is dead."

"What!? How? Where did you . . ."

"In the pond. Drowned. You can't go there. I can't go back."

"How do you know it's Hillary?"

"Small, thin?"

He nodded.

"Black hair?"

He nodded.

"Long red f-f-fingernails?"

His head spun away from her, toward the wall. He gave a kind of cry. Recovering himself with an effort, he grabbed some paper towels from the sink, wiped his face, blew his nose. Then he picked up the telephone receiver again and began to dial. . . .

An hour later, official vehicles were parked helter-skelter all over the long grass in front of the Perry house, shattering the mountain silence with the alien and disconnected clamor of their two-way radios. A Lake Placid ambulance, its pulsing red flashes oddly diminished by the blaze of noon, stood by.

Constable Emmett Wilbur, whose part-time $5,000-a-year post included the privilege of shared office space with the town justice over at the village firehouse, accompanied Littlefield to the pond. They found the body, which Harry duly identified as his wife, Hillary . . . whereupon he fainted dead away. Wilbur, a slight, wiry man of sixty-two, given to donning a gray-green jacket cut along vaguely military lines while in pursuit of the duties of his office, thoughtfully considered the elongated six-foot-three man spread out before him. He decided it would be downright foolish to try to carry him back to the house. Besides, observing him undisturbed during that vulnerable moment of returning to consciousness might offer some insight into his actual feelings about his wife's death. The constable crouched over Harry and did what he could to help him revive.

In time, the two men returned to the house, the larger—ashen-faced, unseeing—firmly supported by the smaller. And although Littlefield didn't know it, the constable's support could henceforth be counted on to extend into other areas, as well. Unscientific though his recent test admittedly had been, Littlefield had passed it with flying colors.

One by one, the vehicles began to depart.

Madeleine sat on the porch steps holding a cup of very strong instant coffee in both her hands to keep it from spilling. She watched, dry-eyed, as the ambulance opened its doors to receive the gurney with its black plastic body bag. There was a dead person in that thing. A woman whose elegant rib cage had been clearly visible on her fashionably thin, cold gray back. Who had she been? Why did she drown? Why did she have to drown *here*? A selfish, uncharitable thought. But the Littlefields weren't supposed to be her problem. She'd come here with a more than an adequate supply of her own.

At last Emmett Wilbur stepped onto the porch with Littlefield.

"May I offer you a lift back into town?" Wilbur asked the other man. "Where will you be staying? Is there anything any of us can do?"

"Uh, no, thank you, Constable. I came in my car—it's parked down there by the road—the gray Cherokee. I've been staying at the Lewises' bed and breakfast."

"Right. The Lewis place. I know it. Nice people . . . are they friends of yours, then? You don't want to be left too much alone just now."

"I've known Don and Betsy for a lot of years. I guess I'll be as well off there as anywhere. . . ." His voice was beginning to lose strength.

Madeleine put down her coffee cup and stood up. She shook Emmett Wilbur's hand, and then briefly touched Littlefield's forearm in a kind of telegraphed gesture of concern.

"Gentlemen," she said. She didn't know what else to say.

"We got word to Rose Bedard, Mrs. Rafferty." Madeleine had told Wilbur about Rose and that Rose had heard Mrs. Littlefield in the barn. "She knows what's happened. She should be back soon with your little girls. Let us know if we can do anything."

"Thank you."

He squinted at a small notebook, holding it out as far his arm would reach, checking over a list. "Oh, and we will need to take a statement from both you and Rose Bedard within the next couple of days."

"Right."

"Well, then, that about wraps things up. Coming, Littlefield? My car's parked right behind yours." Littlefield followed him down the steps, but before proceeding down

64

the driveway, he turned and looked up squarely at Madeleine. He gave her a look that signified they had been through something terrible together. Something both would remember for the rest of their lives. Madeleine acknowledged the look, and then, discomfited, stooped to retrieve her coffee cup. She understood now what it had been about his eyes that had first impressed her. It was their astonishing eloquence.

When Libby and Tillie returned with Rose, they behaved like avid little spectators—too bright-eyed, too brittle with excitement. They understood that something had happened, all right, but seemed to feel only a kind of celebrity from its having happened where they lived. It was, for Madeleine, a sudden reminder of their former Manhattan selves—kids who brought home tales of muggings and gory traffic accidents "right on our street," or "right in front of the building," that were no more real to them, somehow, than the six o'clock news that was the deadly daily backdrop to the hurried preparation of their dinner.

Rose, solemn-faced, walked over to where Madeleine was standing and they exchanged a brief hug.

"Oh, God, Rose, you can't imagine . . . I'm so glad you guys weren't here!"

"Well, it's all over town, of course. Actually, Mrs. Rafferty, for a moment I was afraid it was *you*. It was so awful! All I kept hearing was that something had happened to some woman up at the Perry house. So there I was, trying to shield the girls and still find out what it was, when young Timmy Welch came up to me. God, I used to babysit him, and here he is a full-grown volunteer fireman!"

"Rose, please just call me Madeleine. I don't feel comfortable with that Mrs. Rafferty stuff. As to what's happened, well, I don't want to say too much in front of the girls. I think I may kind of be in shock . . . numb, anyway. It was the worst thing I've ever seen. I was just taking a little walk. I didn't have anything more on my mind than my book. That poor woman! Nobody ought ever to have

65

something like that happen to them . . . to be *seen* like that. . . ."

"Poor Mrs. Littlefield. She wasn't all that bad, really. Just pushy, you know? Went right after whatever it was she wanted. And what she wanted was fast-lane, trendy stuff like the Hamptons, SoHo, *Interview* magazine . . . you know, stuff like that. She hated it up here because it wasn't an 'in' place to be."

"How come you know about SoHo and *Interview* magazine, Rose? Doesn't quite fit that nature-girl image, somehow."

Rose laughed. "Well, thanks a lot! You think I'm some kind of hick, eh? Well, for your information, I've got a BA degree from Oneonta, and I'm certified to teach secondary school art. Not that I ever got around to doing it, what with one thing and another."

Madeleine looked embarrassed. "I guess I haven't figured out *what* to make of you, yet! I just thank God you're here!" The four of them had been milling around the kitchen, putting away the groceries Rose had picked up in town. Now they went out onto the porch. The girls ran to the front of the house and began to play near the steps. Rose and Madeleine sat down on the steps talking quietly.

"Did you see any signs of Hillary Littlefield when you were out there last night?"

"No! I couldn't see a thing. I couldn't even have heard them—whoever it was with her—drive away. The storm was so noisy."

"And the barn door was locked again when you tried it?"

"Yes. Shut tight. That's when I decided to face the music and come here."

"So let's see, that was when—around nine-thirty, ten? By the way, we might as well go over this carefully now, while it's still fairly fresh in our minds, because Constable Wilbur will be taking statements from us."

"I know. Tim said he would. And, yeah, I think it was

around nine-thirty. Did they say what time they think she died?"

"No. Not that I heard, anyway."

"It just doesn't make sense. She was so smart and tough, you know? I kind of admired that about her. What in the world would induce somebody like that to be out there in the middle of one of the worst thunder and lightning storms we ever had around here?"

"Well, look at *you*, Rose. You're smart, and I think you're kind of tough, too. In the best sense of the word. And yet you were out there, too. Very cold and wet, as I recall. And very scared-looking."

"Oh. Well. But the circumstances were so different. I'd been kicked out . . . and I'd lost my key . . . I mean, it was a whole different situation."

"We don't know the situation she was in."

"I guess you're right. I guess we'll just have to wait and see what they find out."

"And listen, Rose . . . help me keep the girls from getting too keyed up about all this, okay? I think we should try to play it down, if at all possible." The girls were already deep into one of their make-believe games.

"C'mon Libby, no fair. You're hogging the game. It's my turn! Lemme be her now. You promised!"

Reluctantly, Libby took the big beach towel that had until recently been hanging from the porch rail to dry and draped it around herself like a cowl.

"Okay!" Tillie said happily. "Now you be the gray ghost and I'll be the drownded lady."

"Oh, good grief, Rose," Madeleine said, rolling her eyes. "It's like they've got these little electronic sensors . . ."

"Bugging us."

"In more ways than one," Madeleine agreed. The lame humor helped, but not much. It was a tragic, eerie situation, and there wasn't a thing they could do to change that. They'd just have to try to muddle through somehow.

Early Monday morning, Madeleine left the mountain and drove into Indian Meadow for her eight o'clock appointment with Constable Wilbur over at the firehouse. Fog still clung to the ground and wood smoke curled up from isolated chimneys. She was wearing a heavy Icelandic sweater, and her breath formed little puffs in front of her face.

Though the investigation had continued on Sunday, it had understandably been centered down the road from them, near the pond. The telephone's loud ring when Wilbur called to set up their appointments had probably been the most startling event of the day. Both she and Rose had jumped a mile.

They arranged for Madeleine to go in first, then Rose. Madeleine had felt the need to put another night's sleep between herself and the events of the day before.

One of the firemen on duty—a burly, personable young fellow with a full red beard—suggested she might want to help herself to coffee.

"You'll find a fresh pot at the end of the hall."

"Thanks." She went down the narrow corridor, following the fragrance to the almost-full glass pot sitting on a burner placed on a small folding table. And there was Harry Littlefield sitting on one of two folding chairs lined up next to the table. He stood up politely when he saw her.

"Hello, Mrs. Rafferty. How has everything been at the house since . . ."

"We're managing, Mr. Littlefield. Rose has been a big help. The children don't really understand, and in a way that's helped to make things seem more . . . well, normal."

"I meant to call to see how you were, but I've practically been living down here since it happened."

Madeleine believed him. That's exactly what he looked like he'd been doing. Brown stubble covered his fine square chin, and his large dark eyes were bloodshot. He had managed a change of clothes at some point—thick soft corduroys and a faded wool Pendleton shirt to ward off the morning chill.

"What have you been able to find out?" And then she wondered whether she was wrong to ask. After all, this was a deeply private crisis; she had no wish to pry. But she needn't have worried. Talking and thinking about it was all that Littlefield could do—all that he had done, in fact, since noon on Saturday.

"They've placed the time of death—pending the coroner's report—at between ten P.M. and midnight Friday. We know she was up here early in the afternoon with a chum of hers from Amagansett. An antiques guy, name of Norbert Mason. Nice enough, in his way. I know him slightly. It seems they were planning to go into business together. First I'd heard of it. See, those toys in the barn were going to be Hillary's entrée. The poor thing thought she was pulling a fast one on me, because the lawyers hadn't come up with a disposition for the contents of the barn. That was so typical of her! By offering them to Mason now, she figured they'd all be gone by the time the lawyers got around to it and it would be a fait accompli. They'd rented a shop in East Hampton. They were going to call it Toys Were Us!" He shook his head slowly in wonder, glumly contemplating the archness of the name.

"They found where she was planning to spend the night. There's a small shed on the property that we converted into a guest cottage. Nothing fancy. We did it the first year so more of her friends could stay here. Hardly ever saw any use. Her overnight bag was there. Looked like she'd just thrown it on the bed and rushed out to meet Mason."

"A guest cottage? I had no idea. I've hardly looked into any of those sheds—" Madeleine interrupted herself, "So that means she knew the main house had been rented?"

"It seems she'd ordered Joe Mitford to find a tenant after I'd told him to hire a caretaker. Poor guy wanted to please us both, but she promised him a very nice commission,

69

which apparently he couldn't resist. His mother keeps him on a tight leash. So he fired Rose and rented the place to you. His instructions had been not to let the rent money go to me, but I guess you went and paid your bill when Joe wasn't around. A royal mess. His mother is furious, as I'm sure Hillary would have been had she ever found out about it." His voice cracked. He took a deep breath. Madeleine didn't say anything.

After a while, Harry continued, "Here I was looking all over for her, and even weird Joe Mitford knew more about her whereabouts than I did! All those friends of hers out in the Hamptons—and not one of them would tell me where she was! It nearly drove me crazy. Why was she so secretive? Did she *need* all that drama? Can you imagine it, Mrs. Rafferty? She'd sworn every one of her friends to absolute secrecy."

"Yes, I think I can imagine it, actually," Madeleine replied. Then she found she couldn't say anything more. Her eyes had filled with tears. She was relieved to find a tissue in the pocket of her jeans.

Constable Wilbur poked his head out of his office and gestured for Madeleine to come in. She sat down, looking around the small room. She spotted a yellowing diploma from Notre Dame University among the carefully framed scenes of trout fishing, but then saw that the name on it was Eugene O'Donnell—that must be the justice who shared this space. A framed letter from some official in Albany was addressed to Constable Emmett Wilbur, however, praising his contribution to some case or other. What was a constable, anyway? And what did a town justice do, for that matter? It seemed so old-fashioned and out of the way.

They settled down to a leisurely conversation. Madeleine didn't have the sense of "being questioned" or "making a statement" at all, although the Constable did take notes while they spoke.

After she'd filled him in on the events of the day of the

storm, Wilbur asked her, "Have you straightened out this business with Joe Mitford in the meantime?"

She assured him that Rose had indeed returned the money the next day—before she'd taken the girls to the lake.

"The Mitfords have been in these parts for so long, they sometimes act as though they own the place. But I like Joe. He does have mighty weird-looking eyes, I'll grant you, but basically he's got a pretty good head on his shoulders. If you ask me, he'd've been a lot better off if he'd left Indian Meadow—and that mother of his—a long time ago. All the rest of that bunch did. Seems to me there were six of 'em, all told."

Wilbur went on to say some very nice—and to Madeleine reassuring—things about Rose and her family. "They're good, hard-working people. Even that boyfriend of hers—the one they're all so upset about."

"You mean Jake Charpentier? What's he like?"

Emmett Wilbur laughed—quite a big laugh to come from such a slight man. "Oh, well, I guess he was wild in his younger days—you know, motorcycles, black leather jackets, long hair, that kind of stuff. A rebellious fellow, you might say. But he never got into serious trouble. I figure he'll be carrying a briefcase and wearing a suit before long. He's a smart young man." He laughed again. Then he sat back and turned his full attention to Madeleine.

"So, Mrs. Rafferty . . ." he said, "what brings you here to Indian Meadow?"

"Oh. Well. I'm here to write a book."

"I know that. But why here?"

"Mmm. I guess it's because Lakeshore Realty had an ad in the *New York Times* the day I looked. I wanted a house in the mountains for six months, and their ad said something about short- and long-term rentals. Simple as that."

"You spoke to Joe Mitford on the phone, did you?"

"Yes. He described the Perry house to me and it

sounded really fine. I could just picture it. Actually, it turned out to be even better than I expected. I think it's the most beautiful place I've ever seen. I just love being there. We all do."

"So. You took it over the phone, and then drove up the very next day with your two little girls and moved in."

"Yep. Just like that."

"Making a big move like that in such a hurry . . . why?"

"I, um, very urgently needed to get away from my husband, Constable." Madeleine's voice sounded weary. She clearly didn't want to get into this.

Emmett Wilbur, who'd been happily married for thirty-five years, seemed to catch the deep pain in her eyes.

"I'm sorry," he said, hurriedly. "I did wonder whether you were expecting him to join you. Tell you the truth, I'd been hoping that he might so you'd have someone with you."

"And why would you want that?"

"Why? Why? Mrs. Rafferty . . . my dear young lady . . ." He took her hand avuncularly. "Don't you see, we don't know how Hillary Littlefield came to drown."

"Wait a minute. I'm not sure I understand. Are you saying it might not have been an accident?"

He nodded slowly and sadly. "I'm sorry to say that possibility does exist. We have no idea where she was before she ended up in that pond. We don't know why she would be outdoors during that terrible storm. We haven't been able to account for her whereabouts from the time her business partner left for Long Island until her death eight hours later.

"So, dear Mrs. Rafferty, until we find out more about what may have happened to Hillary Littlefield . . . well, I would certainly caution you to be very, very careful. At all times. Please."

CHAPTER

8

ON that same cool Monday, early in the afternoon, Sylvie Blaustein received an unexpected visitor at her small house in Port Washington, Long Island.

Something about the person standing on her stoop made her doubtful. Though his features were regular—distinctive, even—and the navy-blue blazer and gray flannel pants were of good cut, the expression on his face made her hesitate. Was this person about to offer her a copy of some religious tract?

"Sylvie!" The voice was smooth, soft, practiced. Its owner obviously counted it among his assets. He gave the impression of somebody whose list of assets had been dwindling lately, like his hairline. "It's Gil Rafferty. How are you? I had a photo shoot over at the yacht club—for Schweppe's, actually—and I thought I'd take a chance and drop by. May I step in for a moment?"

Sylvie automatically looked up at his forehead and saw the small, maroon, five-stitch, cross-hatched scar very close to his right eye. He saw the glance and ignored it. He smiled, and without her actually inviting him to do so, he stepped into the modest foyer.

"I thought you didn't recognize me there at first!"

"Hello, Gil. Yes, I remember you. You came to the Dexter picnic we had here last year. But I don't believe we've met since then, have we?"

"My, has it been as long ago as that?" Gil shook his head incredulously. His confident delivery rang utterly hollow. He looked over her shoulder into the living room, as though hoping she would ask him to come in and sit down. Sylvie did so, in spite of herself. When he walked past her she caught a whiff of day-old whiskey coming through his pores. His breath, on the other hand, was 100-proof Clorets.

"Gil, won't you tell me what this is about? I have to leave for a meeting in a very short time." A lie. She was waiting for Matt to come home; they were going out to dinner and a movie.

"Well, I'm sorry to say that my dear wife of eleven years appears to have left me and taken our children with her. Perhaps Matt already told you this much?" He cleared his throat carefully. There was a trace of fear in his eyes now. *How much has Matt told you?*

"Yes. I know. I understand that Madeleine is no longer working at Dexter. Matt really misses her down there."

Gil cleared his throat again. "I was wondering, ahem, whether you might help me, Sylvie." He coughed. "I'm sorry, I seem to have something caught in my throat."

"Can I get you anything? A cup of coffee?" Sylvie didn't want to be doing this. She wanted him out of her living room. None of the words he was speaking, none of his gestures or expressions rang true. A faint trace of madness hung palpably in the air. And while Sylvie realized that this man—whatever his problems might be—would not do her any harm, she felt compromised, sullied, by his presence and by his ability somehow to encircle her in his own deceit.

When she returned from the kitchen, Gil Rafferty sipped his coffee slowly, holding the good china cup with exaggerated care. "You see, Sylvie, it's like this. Madeleine and I may be through. But I'm still the father of those two little girls. And I don't know where she's taken them. She sublet the apartment to some accountant from Mamaroneck and left without providing so much as a forwarding address."

"Yes. I understand. Matt mentioned that she'd moved out."

"Sylvie, can't you tell me more than that?"

"Really. No. I didn't ask. Matt never said."

"I just want to see my kids, Sylvie. I'm beside myself with worry about those little girls. Sylvie, Madeleine is—how can I put it? She's not in *command* sometimes, you understand? She gets very, very agitated. I'm not sure she's capable of managing alone."

Sylvie was about to stand up and firmly usher Gilbert Rafferty out of her house—she *knew* how well Madeleine had been managing!—when the doorbell rang. It was the paper girl. Monday was when she came round to collect.

While Sylvie went upstairs for her purse, Gil stood up and walked deliberately into the kitchen. For more coffee. Also to see what he could find. A big calendar was hanging next to the wall phone. He studied it for brief seconds, lifting the page back to the month of May. Nothing. He riffled forward to July. Ah. There at the bottom of the page was a jagged marginal scrawl: "Maddie: Indian Meadow, Adirondacks."

Gil took out his wallet and slipped out a small three-by-five glossy of Libby and Tillie at ages four and seven. On the back of this, he wrote, "Indian Meadow, Adirondacks," and then, almost as an afterthought, added, "Elizabeth & Matilda."

He pressed so hard with the nib of his big fat Mont Blanc pen that the ink formed wet black puddles in the loops of the *D*'s and the *A*'s.

He did not bother to write Madeleine's name. This was no longer about her.

When Sylvie stepped back into the living room, she saw Gil just coming back in from the kitchen. He gestured to her with his cup to indicate he had refilled it. He seemed calmer somehow.

Late that evening after the children had gone to bed, Madeleine and Rose sat down together on the porch and analyzed their separate sessions with Constable Wilbur— virtually word by word. Huddled in warm sweaters in the long lingering evening light of early June, they sat watching the sky fade as imperceptibly as a drying watercolor, until at last it was truly dark and they could barely see each other's faces.

"So. What do you think he thinks?" Madeleine said.

"I think he thinks it's possible."

"What?"

"That somebody did it to her."

"But don't you also think he thinks it could've happened without any of that stuff? Just an unfortunate accident owing to the violent storm?"

"Yes. I'm sure that's the way he's looking at it officially. But I got the feeling that he's real uneasy about it in his guts. Madeleine, he told me we should be real careful up here. And he asked me whether Jake will be joining us any time soon."

"He asked me that, too. About my husband, I mean."

"Who else could have been out there that night?" Rose asked.

"Some stranger?"

"Or maybe somebody like Joe Mitford."

"Or Harry Littlefield." Or, Madeleine could not help thinking, Rose.

Once you let yourself think like that, there was no telling where it might lead. Besides, that was the constable's job.

Following things through wherever they might lead. Best just leave it to him, then.

She did not want to be thinking about people killing each other. Her own sense of how it must feel to kill—*a blind swift surge of force, the sick knowledge that it's already over before you even know what you are about to do!*—was still too recent and too painful.

True, the obelisk had not killed Gil. But only by a matter of inches. Of centimeters. Perhaps the merest sliver of a centimeter.

Wasn't that why they'd come all the way up to this achingly beautiful place to begin with? To get away from Gil. To find a safe haven. Some clean and isolated place where Libby and Tillie would not be victimized. Where they could just be children. That's what she'd come looking for. But evidently the world had become so crowded with craziness, it had begun percolating its way up into these hidden backwaters like some malodorous toxic sludge.

Rose asked, "Say, are you okay?"

"Oh. Yes. I guess. I'm sort of upset. I'll work it out. It's just that—"

The phone rang then, its rasping shrillness tearing into the velvety dark like a chainsaw.

"*Oh, my God!* Remind me to turn the volume down on that thing." Madeleine ran to stop it before it rang again and woke the girls.

It was Matt. Madeleine had forgotten to telephone him as she'd promised to do every Monday. She felt guilty, unprofessional.

"So what's the story up there, Maddie? You going native on me, or what?"

"Oh, Matt, I'm so sorry. I promise I'll remember from now on. There've been some distracting things going on. . . ." And then she realized that she couldn't, wouldn't, tell Matt about the death of Hillary Littlefield. It would be one more complication for him to be understanding about, and he'd already been more understanding than she had any right to expect.

"Ah, Maddie, I know you, it's okay. But, um, there's been some stuff going on down here, too, that I felt you should know about." He paused for a minute, and then, with a kind of wry chuckle, he said, "You might say, I've got bad news and bad news . . . which do you want to hear first?"

"Oh, well, in that case, Matt, better let me have the bad."

"Okay. Good choice. Here goes." Another pause. "Now, Maddie, I'm not sure this is anything. I'm only telling you this because Sylvie insisted. But, well, Gil came to the house today. . . ." He gave her the details.

"If Sylvie didn't tell him anything . . . I mean, what do I have to worry about?"

"Sylvie says he went into the kitchen to refill his coffee cup. We have your name and location written in on the calendar. But not on the current page—we have it on the page for July, for when we plan to come up to visit. It'd be a real longshot that he'd've spotted it there. But Sylvie was so upset when she remembered, she insisted on my telling you."

"Oh, God, Matt. It's just the sort of sneaky, perverse thing he'd be capable of." Madeleine's heart sank. She realized that if it wasn't this, sooner or later it would be something else. No matter how careful she was, Gil would eventually manage to find them. It was just a matter of time. They'd have to deal with it, that's all. So much for safe havens. "I just wanted to put as much time and distance between us as I could—for as long as I possibly could."

"Well, you probably still have all kinds of time. If I were you I wouldn't think too much of this. But I thought you'd want to know. Now for the next thing . . ."

"Shoot."

"Maddie, there's gonna be a board meeting on Friday

78

morning. Apparently another one of those confounded takeover rumors. Anyway, our, um, somewhat eccentric arrangement regarding your book may come to light. I've got to cover my tail. Can you let me have two chapters and a complete story plan by Friday? Send it via Federal Express."

"Jesus. Look, whatever it takes, I'll do it. I've got one chapter just about done. I've got a pretty good plot outline already. That just leaves Chapter Two. No sweat. You'll have it by Friday."

"Thanks, kid."

Madeleine hung up. Two crimson splotches had appeared on her cheekbones. "Did you hear that, Rose?"

"I'll keep the kids out of your way. I'll take 'em to the lake if the weather's nice. You'll get it done!"

"Thanks. But I'd best start right now, just in case."

Madeleine sat down at her desk and decided the best thing she could do was simply to bite the bullet and write Chapter Two. If she could get that much out of the way, the other stuff, the outline, the changes and corrections, could be accomplished later. But having formulated this brave plan, she found herself powerless to implement it. She sat there—blank, useless, and ever closer to despair—for nearly an hour.

And then she picked up her green felt-tip pen, and very slowly it began to form words on the yellow legal pad. The story just came . . . yet from such a very great distance, it took everything she had just to receive it and get it down.

When at last she'd finished and crawled blindly into bed, her surrender to sleep was instantaneous. She did not hear the lone hoarse bird already squawking at the first pink beams of sunlight. And though she probably didn't realize it, she'd just spent an intensely happy night.

At around ten that morning, Rose looked into Madeleine's room, saw the raft of pages piled up on her desk, and had enough sense to let her sleep. Madeleine was up at noon, feeling fine.

By noon on Thursday, Madeleine was driving into the village of Indian Meadow. Her work completed, she'd arranged to use the Xerox machine at Lakeshore Realty before shipping the pages off via Federal Express. Mrs. Mitford had positively cooed at the prospect of offering assistance to the writer from New York.

Madeleine hesitated on the stoop of Lakeshore Realty long enough to shift the manila envelope and free her hand to turn the knob. That was all the time it took to hear the raised, angry voices inside. They died down on her entrance with the unerring precision of a maestro's swift baton. Joe, his mother, and Missie Rollins stood in the middle of the shop, their faces now safely rearranged into a welcome. Seeing her, Joe looked up and smiled.

"Ah, Mrs. Rafferty! We were just talking about you!"

Mrs. Mitford, horrified by her son's faux pas, gave an involuntary downward motion of her hand. That baton again.

"What Joseph means, Mrs. Rafferty, is that we were discussing some arrangements made before your arrival. Nothing whatsoever to do with you.

"I've asked Missie here to assist you with your photocopying. But before you get on with that, I did want to express my most heartfelt regret about the dreadful drowning at the pond. I can't tell you how upset I was to hear of it. Nobody has ever perished in that pond before—never! Not in all the years I've lived here, and never before that, either, as far as anyone can say. Such a terrible, terrible thing. Poor, poor Mrs. Littlefield! We didn't even know she was in the vicinity. Still such a young woman—hardly out of her twenties. And poor Mr. Littlefield, too! Such a decent man. Truly a tragedy."

Madeleine stood there listening and nodding, watching Joe studying his feet while his mother held forth. Then he looked up and their eyes met (so to speak).

80

"Thank you for your concern," Madeleine said. "I appreciate it. It has been terrible. But I still have this work to do, you see, and maybe that's a blessing. So I guess I'll just get on with it, if I may. Thank you again." She followed Missie Rollins to the back room.

Today Missie was wearing a curiously dated outfit that made her look like an aging California hippie—brightly patterned polyester shirt with a long pointy collar, a long leather vest, several strings of multicolored beads, and strangely cut, unflattering "designer" jeans. She turned to Madeleine and said, "They really weren't talking about you, you know. Those two are always at it. Joe keeps trying to pull these little deals over on her, but she keeps catching him at it. Hmph. Men." She patted the large pale blond bun on the top of her head, checking to make sure that the leather thong securing it was still in place, and turned to look expectantly at Madeleine, who felt no need to reply. Madeleine was noticing how Missie's wiry gray hairs, combed in among the blond ones, seemed ready at any moment to spring out of their tight confinement and escape that odd round doughnut altogether.

She stood there, off to one side, admiring the way Missie proceeded to speed through the formidable stack of papers with mindless ease.

Missie's large freckled hands, however competent, had a tendency to sweat. Damp dimples puckered the freshly processed 8½-by-11-inch sheets, still warm from the Xerox machine, as she went about placing them in orderly piles. "There. All done."

"Missie, I don't know how to thank you. What would I have done without you?" All the while thinking, Oh, please God, don't let me end up like this poor unfortunate woman.

"Well, actually, there is something. . . ." Missie, hearing the opening she'd been waiting for, replied rather too quickly. "A teensy favor I've been dying to get up the nerve to ask you—ever since I heard you were a writer. You see, I also write."

"Really?" Madeleine asked, groaning inwardly.

"Oh, just some jottings, I guess you'd call them." A modest self-conscious titter. "But . . . it's what I live for, truly! If it weren't for my journals, well, I don't know how I should ever have survived the ugliness of my recent divorce." She stepped closer, close enough for Madeleine to smell her stale coffee breath. Strong coffee, and too much of it, plus something vaguely acidic and medicinal. Here it came then, the question anyone connected with publishing, however tangentially, most dreads to hear: "Could you possibly find it in your heart to look at my little manuscript?" Missie's pale watery blue eyes flashed diamond hard.

What could Madeleine say? She'd been trapped and she knew it. What's more, Missie, damn her, knew it, too.

"Why, Missie! What a surprise. I'd be delighted to look it over."

Missie simpered with pleasure.

Madeleine left the chapters for the Federal Express pick up and stepped wearily out into the mild early-afternoon sunshine.

She crossed the Promenade to where her car was parked, already dreading Missie's awful—no doubt about that!—manuscript. She thought nostalgically of those first pristine days on the mountain, when her thin, new "to do" folder had promised such a pure new life. What was it about her that repeatedly attracted the Missie Rollinses of this world? What did they see in her face that gave them the courage to impose? And why did she cave in so easily to their pathetic needs? When she reached her car, there was Joe Mitford standing by it. Another one.

"Ah, there you are, Mrs. Rafferty. I thought this might be your car. I wanted to apologize, you know, for that, um, awkward moment in there. Really, we weren't talking about you. It just came out wrong when I said that. I meant we'd just been talking about the Perry house. You know, about Rose and why I let her go. My mother is cross with me. She didn't know I'd hired Rose, so she was real disturbed to learn I'd fired her. I mean—"

"Joe, it's okay, really. Don't give it another thought. Look, I'm really kind of bushed. I just want to get back to that pretty house and cool my heels."

She saw his face tense up at the dismissal in her voice. Well, damn it, she *was* tired. She'd make it up to him another time.

Joe stepped back to let her enter the car. Madeleine got behind the wheel, waved, and pulled away from the curb. As she drove down the Promenade and out of the village, her rearview mirror continued to reflect the solitary figure of Joe Mitford standing at the curb, growing smaller and smaller.

And there he remained for quite some time, his odd eyes continuing to scan the vacant street long after her car had completely disappeared from view.

CHAPTER

9

VERY late that night, Joe Mitford again stood alone, in much the same attitude: very still, scanning the absolute dark. It was past two o'clock in the morning, and he was on the steps of the Mitford front porch. He had not had any sleep. *Out till all hours!* Night after night. Why was this happening?

Was this something he ought to have told Constable Wilbur? It was so embarrassing. To risk exposing the family to the harsh, judgmental eyes of ignorant strangers!

And what if it turned out to have been something else after all? Their lives would be in ruins regardless. Shattered. Nothing would ever be the same.

On the other hand, what if what happened to the odious Hillary Littlefield were to happen again? Only this time to the kind and beautiful Madeleine Rafferty? He couldn't bear the thought. Oh, please let this all be a bad dream.

But Joe's growing fatigue only underlined the truth of the matter. He was not asleep. It was not a dream.

*　　*　　*

As it happened, Joe Mitford would feature in Constable Wilbur's thoughts that very morning—Friday. Now, nearly a week since the discovery of the body in Little Quaker Pond, he'd received his copy of the coroner's report from the county sheriff's office. It contained no unexpected findings. Estimated time of death remained between ten P.M. and midnight. He would have been gratified to learn of some irregularity, no matter how small. Say, the presence of drugs or alcohol. Negative. Or a pregnancy. Negative. Or any other indication that might suggest some impairment to her reputed good judgment. Nothing.

Hillary Littlefield's injuries—contusions, abrasions, two broken collar bones, multiple fractures of both arms and one hand, a smashed-up knee, several broken ribs, with the concomitant bruising and puncture of various internal organs—were consistent with what had happened to her. The severity of these multiple injuries might indeed have killed her, but had not.

She had drowned. She had drowned very soon upon mis-stepping into the mountain brook that had been swollen by rain that night into a fierce, raging current whose force and rapidity had simply overwhelmed her. She was carried along over rocks and boulders and the carcasses of old fallen trees for about half a mile—a journey of no more than a minute or two. Until she reached an abandoned beaver dam, which halted her progress and caused the battered "healthy, slightly malnourished, five-foot-four, 103-pound female Caucasian" to reach her ultimate resting place in the cold black water at the entrance to the pond.

No, there had been no surprises. The constable had been treating the Littlefield case as an accidental death all along. There had never been anything of substance to suggest that it was anything else. No footprints. No evidence whatsoever that somebody had been chasing her. If such footprints had once existed, the pouring rain had certainly succeeded in washing every last one of them away. People had been interviewed at length. All had been candid and reasonably clear as to their whereabouts.

Norbert Mason had left Indian Meadow to return to Long Island that day at around three, with Hillary's promise to provide him with a complete inventory of the toys by early the next week.

Rose Bedard—who'd actually been outside on the Perry house property during the storm—had seen nothing unusual. She had been able to confirm that Mason and Hillary Littlefield had indeed been present at the barn early that afternoon. Her story was complicated and a bit dramatic, but for the life of him, Wilbur could not find reason to suspect Rose of pushing Hillary Littlefield into the brook.

But where had Hillary Littlefield spent the hours from three in the afternoon until the time of her death? In that tiny guest cottage that had shown absolutely no sign of use? That hardly seemed possible.

Nobody had seen her or heard her. This was no outdoor girl. She was not one to have suddenly gone off on a hike. Especially not with a storm threatening. If she'd stopped at a local restaurant for dinner, her visit had completely escaped notice. This didn't seem possible. He personally remembered how everything about Hillary Littlefield's entire being had screamed for attention. Nor did she have car trouble. Her new maroon Audi had been found parked well off the road, up from the Perry place, in perfect running order.

Madeleine Rafferty had gone to the toy barn later that afternoon, toward five, with her two little girls. They'd sat out part of the storm there. They'd seen nobody. Heard nothing but the storm.

Harry Littlefield had spent the evening with the Lewises, playing bridge with another of their guests, a man whose wife had preferred to watch television. They were all in the big wood-paneled lounge when the electricity went. The game continued by candlelight, and everybody went to bed around midnight. Littlefield had no idea, at that time, that his wife was within fifty miles of Indian Meadow. He found out from Rose the next morning, whereupon he'd driven straight up to the Perry house.

Everybody had been spoken to—even the man and his wife who had preferred television to bridge. They'd been especially difficult to locate as they had been on their way to Montreal to visit a niece whose name nobody knew.

Emmett Wilbur had spoken to Joe Mitford because of the complications surrounding Rose's job as caretaker: her abrupt dismissal and subsequent "squatting" on the property. Peculiar circumstances, yes, but all explained in a manner that made them understandable when you knew the people involved. And Wilbur did. He'd been here over six years, now. Living here contentedly with his small "early retirement" pension from those hard, struggling years as a corrections officer at Dannemora, his salary as constable, and Harriet's bit of income from her nature stories. Lots of people did that up here. Putting little jigsaw pieces of income together, making do, just for the sheer pleasure of living in this beautiful country. They'd been the happiest years of his life, so far. He owed it to this community to make sure there was no more to this Littlefield drowning than the superficial facts would indicate.

Emmett Wilbur simply did not believe that it was possible for folks to disappear in the woods around Indian Meadow. For a couple of hours, maybe. But eight or nine? No, there was too much incidental traffic in these parts nowadays. Too many cars parked by the sides of the road, license plates from all over. Campers. Hikers. Bikers. Tourists. If Hillary Littlefield had gone anywhere, sooner or later somebody would have seen her. And he would have heard about it.

Had somebody lied to him?

And that was when the Constable found himself thinking about Joe Mitford again. He thought he remembered a point during their talk together when those unsettling blue eyes of Joe's had briefly seemed to belie his words.

When had that been? And what had they been talking about at the time?

After all the hard work involved in getting Matt's material off to him, Madeleine felt she'd earned a break. Which was why, not long after Harry Littlefield had departed for Quogue to attend a memorial service for his wife, Madeleine, Rose, Libby, and Tillie all piled into the car and headed for Essex, New York, a stately stone and brick hamlet on the shores of Lake Champlain. Here, they boarded the ferry to Vermont, from whose deck the ancient, massive Adirondack range suddenly loomed steeper and more hugely monumental than they'd ever seen it. And on the opposite shore, the jagged, intricate, endless expanse of the much younger Green Mountain range soared into the clouds above the lush Champlain Valley. The short ride across white-capped, windswept fresh water, noisy with the sharp cries of gulls and the rhythmic snap of flags straining at their halyards, took on a ceremonial air. Crossing this exhilarating divide together seemed to Madeleine to have united them in some special, auspicious way.

She could feel herself regaining perspective. The shock of Hillary Littlefield's awful accident had begun to recede. When they got back, she'd be able to deal with her *own* problems again. Those were enough for any one person. Hillary Littlefield was not her problem. Gilbert Rafferty was. Writing a novel was. She'd get on with it.

They drove up through Burlington and visited Rose's family in their beautiful but crumbling old country house outside Winooski. Rose had been pining to see her children—a pair of lean, leggy, black-eyed boys, barely a year apart, and their two-year-old, auburn-haired baby sister. Whatever strain existed between Rose and her parents was, thanks to the Raffertys' buffering presence, put aside for the day, which was exactly what Rose had had in mind.

They didn't return to Indian Meadow until long after dark. A cold wind had blown in from the north. When Madeleine's headlights disclosed the familiar line of trees by the Perry house driveway, the branches were bending and swaying almost to the ground.

Libby and Tillie had long since fallen asleep in the backseat. Not much had been heard from the passenger seat either. It must have been a tough day for Rose: first the delight of seeing her children, then the wrench of saying good-bye again. Giselle, her cherubic little girl, had stolen Madeleine's heart. How could Rose bear to leave her behind? Children changed so quickly at that age. She remembered when Libby and Tillie were two . . . how she'd fussed over every little accomplishment, every new word. Had she been a bit obsessive? Maybe Rose had the right idea, after all. People were so different. Rose seemed content just to deal with things as they came. Besides, they'd all be together again soon. From a conversation she'd tried hard not to appear to overhear, Madeleine sensed Jake Charpentier's return from Canada was imminent.

"Looks like we've had a change in the weather."

"Ah, you're awake. I thought you'd drifted off."

"Maybe, for a little bit. Brrr, it's cold! Will you look at those trees!" The temperature had dropped to the low forties. Higher up on the mountain, there would probably be frost.

They carried the girls inside, got them into their pajamas, to the bathroom, and into bed without their quite waking. Madeleine took a pair of extra blankets from the linen closet and covered them both. To think that very afternoon they'd been splashing half-naked in the Bedard family's duck pond!

Then she and Rose went around closing windows. Madeleine decided she also needed another blanket and was closing the door to the linen closet when Rose came out of the bathroom.

"Wonder whatever became of that gray blanket? The

one you took that other cold night? Is it still in the laundry shed, or what?"

Rose, half asleep, stopped, looking at Madeleine as though she hadn't heard right.

"The what?"

"That gray blanket. One of the first nights we were here. Remember? It got real cold, just like this. Before we met. You, well, came in and took one of the blankets out of the linen closet. Tillie caught sight of you just as you were leaving." She laughed, remembering, "We called you the gray ghost."

Rose's tired eyes widened.

"You what? Tillie what? Madeleine, I don't know what you're talking about. I never took anything from this house. Ever. First of all, I wouldn't. That's not how I was raised. And second of all, I couldn't have. I told you, I didn't have a key to the main house. How could you think I would do such a thing?" Tired as she was, Rose was furious. Furious and disillusioned.

"Jesus Christ, Madeleine, here I invite you to spend the day with my family, and you turn around and accuse me of stealing a blanket right out from under your nose! What do you think I am? Some low, no-account redneck?"

A sharp gulf suddenly yawned between them. What had she done? Madeleine wondered. She didn't care about the blanket. She had just been reminiscing, thinking about how far they'd come. How fragile her hold on this newfound existence was, after all. *And if Rose didn't take a blanket that night . . . that meant it must have been somebody else!* Madeleine felt as though everything might just collapse around her.

"Rose, I'm *sorry*! It wasn't an accusation. Not at all. Hell, if I'd been out in the cold that night, I sure would have borrowed a blanket if I could have. Honest. I was just putting myself in your place. It seemed a perfectly okay thing to do in the circumstances."

"Well, I don't know how it is down in New York, where

90

you come from, but where I come from people are taught to respect one another's property."

"Please, Rose. We're both tired. If I'd've known how offended you'd be, I never would have said anything. Somebody did break in that night. Now I'm wondering who it really was. All these weeks, I'd just assumed it was you. I didn't think any more of it. I mean, one lousy blanket, big deal. There's a dozen more in here."

"Come to think of it, I do remember that night. I about froze to death. I'd draped every piece of clothing I owned around me. Maybe you're right. Maybe, if I'd had a key, I *would* have tried to take something from the house to help me keep warm. I don't know. I guess I am tired. It seemed like . . . well, like you were looking down on me, you know? Sometimes I think you just put up with me because you think I'm like this 'quaint backwoods character,' you know?"

Madeleine went over and hugged her.

"Now, cut that out. Please. We're friends. I bet we know each other for the rest of our lives. You're very, very tired. I can imagine how emotional today must have been for you. Those kids of yours are *terrific!*"

Rose's tight, drawn face softened at last.

"Yeah," she said, "they are, aren't they?"

"Go to bed. Get some sleep. I'll see you tomorrow."

Madeleine piled the extra blanket on her bed, got in between the chilled, inhospitable sheets, turned off the light, and waited for her body heat to spread its warmth. She was much, much too tired to give any further thought to who their actual intruder might have been.

CHAPTER

10

IT would be several days before Madeleine thought about their intruder again. The next morning, she sat down at her typewriter right after breakfast, prepared to resume work at full throttle. And almost from the start, she realized her story was in trouble.

Why, if she was supposedly in charge, couldn't she make these characters do what the conventions of the romance formula required them to do? They'd dug in their heels, refusing to move the story forward. She had to come up with something.

Every morning, Madeleine would watch Rose take the girls off on outings to the lake or the woods or the riding stable, promising herself she'd join them again before long. Just as soon as Chapter Three sorted itself out. Scratching idly at the painful, lumpy black fly bites on her legs, and spraying herself liberally with insect repellent, she'd sit down once again at her typewriter on the porch. What if she wasn't going to be able to bring this story off after all?

On Friday, just before dawn, she was awakened by a

strangely vivid dream about Lena, the girl whose death she'd "seen" that stormy night in the barn and written into the story soon after. That had been a mistake. Her book still needed her. She would bring Lena back. That felt right.

Strange! Why had Lena's death seemed so irrevocable to her that night? Might she have been responding to something in the atmosphere, some sort of precognition of the actual death about to occur? Nonsense. With a wave of her green felt-tip pen, Madeleine gave Lena Zane a second chance at life. More, alas, than anyone could do for Hillary Littlefield.

She went into the kitchen, made coffee, and took a fresh, steaming cupful out to the porch. It was going to be a beautiful day.

She sat on the steps, listening to the waking birds, watching the shadows melt in the rosy, golden light, seeing the outlines of the field and sheds beyond it come into sharp focus. God, she loved this place! When the long grass by the edge of the woods had become its bright, clear daytime green, she noticed an object lying on the ground. She put down her cup and walked through the wet grass to have a closer look. It was an old-fashioned wooden badminton racquet and, lying next to it like some poor dead bird, an abandoned shuttlecock composed of real white feathers glued in a stiff jaunty circle around the red rubber tip.

It was the croquet set all over again.

Somebody was taking toys from the barn and leaving them outside. She remembered how upset Joe had been that first morning to see the croquet set left outside.

Madeleine picked the racquet up—there was just the one, no partner to this peculiar crime, apparently. It was a lovely old thing, painted in red and green and black concentric stripes with the manufacturer's name—W. J. Hargreaves and Sons, Fall River, Mass.—emblazoned in florid script. She stooped again to pick up the shuttlecock and, batting it lightly up and down on the racquet, returned to her half-finished coffee on the porch steps.

Her coming out this morning must have caught whoever it was unawares. Their gray ghost? Something worse? It seemed silly to feel threatened on such a beautiful fresh morning. An old badminton racquet. A puzzlement. She'd meant to inform Constable Wilbur about the missing gray blanket after that set-to the other night with Rose, but she had forgotten. Well, she'd do it today without fail.

By eight-thirty, she was at her table on the porch, writing Lena back into the story. Rose and Libby and Tillie, each wearing a backpack, had already gone trotting off down the road. They were going on a hike today, following the blazed trail up their mountain, carrying an ample picnic lunch with which to celebrate the completion of their 3,478-foot ascent to the summit.

Madeleine had barely inserted the second sheet of paper into her typewriter when she had a creepy, prickling sense that she was not alone. She looked up and saw Missie Rollins stepping through the high grass with care, making her way slowly up the slight incline from the drive. She wore a tight primrose-yellow T-shirt with a short pink and green golfing skirt that called unwarranted attention to pale middle-aged thighs.

"Oh, *good*!" She called, "I've caught you at home. I thought I'd take a chance and stop by on my way to work." She drew up to the porch steps and sat down with a great sigh. The walk from the driveway seemed to have exhausted her. Madeleine caught the whiff of stale, strong coffee. "I have my manuscript with me. . . . I brought it along just in case. You did say you'd look at it?"

But she wasn't carrying anything that Madeleine could see.

"How nice," Madeleine said.

"I left it in my car. I didn't know whether you were at home, you see."

"Right. Well, why don't I just walk to your car with you, then, Missie? That will spare you a second trip."

"Oh . . . would you? That's be ever so nice."

It was some two hundred yards to the driveway, and another fifty or so to where Missie's small white late-model Cadillac was parked by the side of the road. It was one of those fussy, overaccessorized hybrids with a fake leather top, the sort of model that Detroit, in its inscrutable marketing wisdom, referred to as "European-style." It had California plates. By the time they drew alongside it, Missie seemed seriously out of breath. She opened the trunk and withdrew a medium-sized suitcase. Now it was Madeleine's turn to gasp. She could see it was heavy. She'd expected something lengthy, but this was ridiculous. It was one of those oxblood-colored composition suitcases college kids once used to ship their laundry home.

"Well, here they are, then. My babies. Guard them with your life!" Missie opened the case, revealing many, many, *many* spiral notebooks. Dog-eared. Coffee-cup circles on the covers. The pages grown fat and pulpy from too many spills, too many turnings.

Missie faced Madeleine close up, her pale eyes pleading. "I just *know* there's something of value here. All it requires is the discernment of a gifted editor, someone who knows what really matters in life . . . someone, Mrs. Rafferty, like *you* . . . I just *know*—" She couldn't go on. The emotion of the moment was too great. She turned and fastened the case closed again.

Madeleine had already decided that she would hold on to the notebooks for a polite length of time and return them unread. The woman was a total fruitcake.

"Right, then." Madeleine turned to go, the heavy case barely fitting under her arm. There was no handle—just an old gray woven strap buckled around its bulging middle.

Missie paused before entering her car.

"It's so lovely to see this dear old place again. I haven't been by here since I got back last month."

"Oh. From California?"

"Yes. Twenty years it's been. My marriage broke up, you know . . ."

"Mmm. So you said. Well, this is pretty heavy, Missie. Thanks for, uh—stopping by. I'll get back to you, okay?"

"Oh, no, no. It is *I* who must thank *you*!"

The first thing Harry Littlefield did when he got back to Indian Meadow was touch base with Emmett Wilbur. It didn't surprise him much to learn there was nothing new to report.

"I'm staying on it, Harry. There's this long gap of time where we just don't know where your wife was or what she was doing."

"Somebody must have seen her."

"Let's hope so. Because if somebody did, I'll find out about it."

"Uh, look, Emmett. There's something else I wanted to ask you about. I've been staying over at the Lewises' now for over two weeks, and, well, it's just not a good situation. I mean, they're set up for weekenders, overnight vacationers, people out to enjoy themselves. And there I am, holed up as if it were some kind of boarding house or something, trying to deal with this awful mess. I'm starting to trip all over myself."

"And?"

"And, I was wondering how it would sit with you if I just bunked in that guest cottage up at my place until this all gets settled."

"Have you spoken with Mrs. Rafferty about this?"

"Oh, no. Not without talking to you first. She may object, of course. But that cottage is really tucked away. You can't even see it from the main house."

"I wish you would, Harry. It'd make me feel a whole lot

better about those two women living there alone. Why don't you go ask 'em?"

"Yeah. Okay, I will. Hell, all she can say is no."

"Being up there won't bother you any?"

"You mean, because of what happened. . . ."

"Might bring it all back."

"I've got to deal with it sooner or later, Emmett. Going to that memorial service out on the Island helped a lot. Gave me perspective. There was a huge turnout. People out there really loved her. God knows, I did, too. But she could be difficult. Hell, who am I kidding? She could be impossible. Often was. Like when we were up here in Indian Meadow. You wouldn't have exactly called her popular around here, would you?"

The constable merely grunted in vague agreement.

"Emmett, my wife and I didn't get along. I'm trying to get over her death as best I can; I'd like to think maybe I could help clear up how she came to drown like that. I mean, what if somebody else *was* involved? When Hillary was feeling ugly, well, there's no telling how she might cross somebody. I think . . . if there is anything at all still to be learned up there at the Perry House, maybe my being right on the property could help smoke it out."

"You don't have to persuade me, Harry. I'm in favor of it. Go ask Madeleine Rafferty. Like you said, all she can say is no." When Littlefield showed no sign of getting up to go, Emmett Wilbur finally understood what was really being asked of him.

"Ah-ha. Now I get it. You want me to go with you, eh? . . . Give it my, um, official seal of approval. That it?"

"It sure would help. I think."

Madeleine just dropped Missie's heavy case in a corner on the porch and left it. It was too heavy and too problematic to waste time over. Now that she knew where her story was going again, she begrudged any interruption. But she'd

97

no sooner "unwritten" Lena's dramatic death scene than she saw the constable's car drive up.

With some dismay, she watched as both Emmett Wilbur and Harry Littlefield stepped out of the car. A delegation! Once the polite exchanges had been accomplished, Littlefield cleared his throat and began—with an occasional assist from Constable Wilbur—to offer his modest proposal.

Although Madeleine appeared to be listening closely, she'd somehow got it into her head that he had come here to evict them. Not all that unthinkable under the tragic and unusual circumstances. But the idea of having to leave came as such a wrenching shock, filled her with such a fearful sense of dislocation, that by the time he'd finished speaking his piece, she'd only just begun to grasp what he'd actually been saying. She replied tentatively, "The guest cottage . . . I've never even looked at it."

"You can't see it from here. It's up beyond the old tool shed."

"I was just wondering whether it's enough for you. Does it have everything you'd need?"

"Oh, yes. It's completely equipped. I put all that stuff in myself some years back. For guests. We never did use it much."

"It just feels odd. I mean, *this* is your house. I feel like an interloper. You never even knew it was being offered for rent. . . ." If she kept this up she just might succeed in getting herself evicted after all.

"Yes, but my wife did. There's no question about that, Mrs. Rafferty. I have no need of this house right now. But I'd like to be nearby. I have to confer with my lawyer and my accountant, see what they recommend me to do about this place. I have a lot of personal things to get through. That cottage would suit me just fine." When she still didn't say anything, he continued, "If it's a matter of the rent you paid, I'd be willing to make any adjustment in that regard you felt appropriate."

98

"*No,* Mr. Littlefield. It's not that. Not at all."

Uh-oh, Emmett Wilbur thought, he's digging himself into a hole.

Harry said, "Excuse that. It wasn't meant the way it sounded."

Emmett stepped in. "Mrs. Rafferty, as you know, I'm in favor of this. For my own reasons. I've felt all along that you and Rose are too isolated up here. Why not let Harry move in for a few days on a trial basis? Then, if anybody's unhappy with the arrangement, he'll just go find something else. Hmm? How about it?"

"Well, Constable, when you put it that way, it sounds quite reasonable."

They shook hands on it.

"Actually, I was meaning to call you about something funny that seems to be going on here." She told them about the blanket incident and the badminton equipment she'd found that morning.

"Why didn't you tell me this before?"

"Well, until the other night, I'd been assuming all along it was Rose."

"Yes, of course. I see."

"And the badminton racquet was just this morning. See, I've still got it here on the porch." She picked it up and handed it to the constable.

"A beauty. That barn is an amazing place."

"It's certainly been there long enough." Harry, standing there by the porch, looking out over his fields and the mountains in the distance, was finding the thought of selling less appealing. "You know, if I do decide to keep this place, I ought to unload those toys. Hillary was right about that. Even with those old storage cabinets, they're starting to deteriorate. Hell, pretty soon they won't be in any shape to be of use to anybody. I should find a dealer, somebody who understands their value and can do right by them."

"Well, the girls sure enjoy playing out there. Rose and I try to see that they treat those things with respect."

Madeleine had a fleeting image of Libby and Tillie fighting over the baby doll like crazed terriers.

"Listen, that's fine. While you're here, please feel free to use the barn whenever you like. I mean that. You people just go on living here the way you have been. I promise to stay out of your way."

"Well, thanks."

"I'd like to pursue this 'intruder business' with you in more detail, Mrs. Rafferty," Emmett added. "Could you come down and give me a complete rundown? Say, tomorrow?"

They made a date for three o'clock Saturday afternoon, and the two men drove off. Emmett felt that something useful had been accomplished. Whether Madeleine's intruder developed into anything or not remained to be seen. But it was certainly more than he'd had when they'd started out that morning.

CHAPTER
11

LIBBY and Tillie and Rose sat on a broad, smooth ledge of sunlit rock at the summit of Stoddard Mountain, eating their sandwiches. Never had Swiss cheese, tomato, and beansprouts on whole wheat tasted so good! They drank cold Red Zinger tea and bit into tart, crisp apples, chewing slowly, looking out over Blue Mirror Lake—which appeared to be not water at all, but some kind of shimmering, glistening precious metal.

Rose hadn't been up Stoddard in years, and she commented on how the trail seemed to have deteriorated—probably a combination of weathering and overuse. There'd been one rather steep stretch, near the top, surfaced with loose, crumbling rock, that had required some tricky hand-over-hand maneuvering. She'd worried that Tillie wouldn't be able to keep up. But the agile little five-year-old had scrambled along on all fours like a cheerful monkey, with no fear at all.

For today, at least, they had the summit to themselves. They savored their exclusivity. Although the house was not visible to them—to glimpse it, one of them would have had to dangle all the way out over the edge, her legs held fast by the other two—their road was, a thin brown ribbon winding its way through the trees.

As Rose crumpled up their sandwich bags and stashed them into her pack to dispose of later, she watched Emmett Wilbur's car heading toward town. She couldn't tell whose it was. They lay down in the sun, heads resting on their backpacks, dozing awhile before starting the trek back down.

Libby, playing lazily with a plump pine cone she'd picked up along the trail, said, "I wish we could just stay here forever. It's so beautiful! I could build us a little hut, and we'd gather nuts and berries and never go back to civilization."

"Sounds like you've got the makings of a real mountain man, honey. I know just how you feel. But don't you think your mommy would worry about you after a while?"

"Oh, she'd be with us, wouldn't she?" Tillie asked.

"Mmm. Yeah, I guess," Libby said. "But she never has time. She's always got all this important work to do."

"Well, if we lived off the land, then she wouldn't have to anymore, would she?"

Rose chuckled. She couldn't fault the logic of that. Where did they get expressions like "Living off the land" from, anyway? Television?

"Okay. Mommy can live here, too."

"And Daddy, too. We'll all live up here together and be happy."

Libby sat up with a start and threw the pine cone she'd been holding out over the edge of the cliff with all her strength. It fairly flew. They could hear it clattering down, taking some pebbles with it.

"*No!*" she said. "No way. We're only having good people."

"I miss Daddy!" Tillie insisted loyally, her eyes filling with tears. "You and Mommy are so mean to him."

Rose, torn between wanting to hear Libby's reply—Madeleine had never confided what had gone wrong in her marriage—and wanting to forestall a full-scale crying scene, hesitated.

And then to her dismay, it was Libby who began to sob. "You don't know! You wouldn't say that if you did. You're too young. Oh, please, Rose. Don't let him come. He's awful. I hate him! I don't ever want to see him again." She rushed over to Rose, burying her face in her shoulder.

Rose had been totally unprepared for this outburst. Helplessly, she patted Libby's back. "Hey, it's okay, babe. It's *okay*. Don't cry. What's wrong? Can't you tell me?"

Libby didn't cry for long. Just a minute or two. She seemed as surprised by her sudden storm as Rose was. She took off her glasses with their bright red frames, wiped her eyes, blinking in the clear glaring light of the mountaintop. It made Rose's heart lurch to see the expression in those naked, unprotected eyes. She helped Libby stand up and gently replace the eyeglasses on the bridge of her straight little nose. Then Rose gave Libby a crushing bear hug, and said, "Honey, don't you know by now that there's nothing so bad you can't tell me or Mommy about it?"

Libby's reply was muffled in Rose's soft chest. It sounded as though she said, "I did. Mommy knows . . ."

And then she pulled away, looking up at Rose with an odd, not-quite-believable smile. "I'm okay now. I'm sorry about crying like that. I don't want to talk about it anymore."

"You're sure?"

"Uh-huh. C'mon, Tillie, I'll race you down." And she began to run, with Tillie rushing after as fast as her small legs could carry her.

"Hey, wait a minute, you guys! It's a long way down. You've got to *pace* yourselves!"

By the time they all three trooped noisily onto the back steps and into the kitchen, Libby's mood had completely recovered. She and Tillie tumbled all over themselves telling Madeleine about the fun they'd had.

"You can see *everything*! And there's nobody around for miles and miles. It's like you owned the *world*!"

"And getting up is a whole different kind of fun from coming down!"

"You know, that's exactly how I've always felt about it, too." Rose laughed, explaining to Madeleine in a proud, indulgent, "you had to be there" tone of voice, "You either love hiking up mountains right from the start, or you hate it. Looks to me like you've got yourself a pair of naturals here! Maybe we'll try one of the High Peaks next. Nipple Top's not far from here; that's a good one. We could even do Mt. Marcy—that's the highest of the High Peaks." Libby and Tillie had begun to giggle at "Nipple Top" and heard no more of Rose's instructive discourse. She said, "Well, that's its name. It looks like, um, just what you think." Then she laughed, too.

"And maybe I'll just join you when you go up Nipple Top!" Madeleine said, giggling a little herself. "I solved that problem with my story today. Of course," she added, "I had to bring somebody back from the dead to do it. I'll bet you guys didn't know I could do that, huh?"

Later, when they were setting the table for dinner, Madeleine said to Rose, "Oh, guess what else happened while you were up on your mountain. . . . Harry Littlefield moved in to the guest cottage."

"What?!"

"Yep. Moved in about an hour ago." Madeleine filled in the rest of the story while they ate.

Rose didn't find a chance to mention Libby's disturbing outburst until after the girls had gone to bed. They were sitting on the porch, enjoying the mild clear night. Rose had brought out the sweater she'd begun to knit for Jake. As she expected, Madeleine was upset to hear about it.

"Oh, God, Rose. Poor Libby. Of course, she's always had a such a terrible temper . . . actually, they both do."

"I've noticed," Rose said gently.

"I'll have to talk to her." She hesitated a moment, and then went on. "Rose, as I'm sure you've gathered by now, we're all of us up here to get away from my husband . . . their father. He's, um, an alcoholic, I'm afraid, and he uses other drugs, too. Cocaine, for one. I still can't believe some of the things he put us through . . . that I sat still for. Now that we've come up here, I know we can manage just fine on our own. We're going to be all right. But if he were to come up here looking for them, well, I wouldn't put it past him to try to make off with them. He's not to be allowed anywhere near them without my being present, okay? I'm telling you this just in case—" The screen door creaked, and they both jumped.

"Mom, I'm hungry. Could I have some cookies and milk, please?" Libby, cozy and cuddly in her pretty pink pajamas, padded out on the porch barefoot and jumped onto Madeleine's lap.

They sat like that, Madeleine's arms hugging her tight, for quite a spell, and then Rose said, "Libby, you're in luck. I just happen to be on my way to the kitchen for a glass of milk myself. Come with me. Madeleine, I think I'll be going on up to bed, after that, okay? See you in the morning."

"Thanks, Rose. For everything. Good night, then. Sleep tight."

When Rose had described the scene on the mountain to her, Madeleine could suddenly picture the expression on Libby's face. It was a look that seared the heart. Unwitting, uncomprehending pain. Ruined innocence. And she had seen it. On one of Gil's photographs. Libby had been standing all alone, looking straight at the camera. Something about that picture had been so terrible. She'd managed only the briefest possible glance before turning it facedown. Thank god, she'd destroyed them all forever. *Dear, sweet Libby, whatever it takes, I'll make it up to you! I promise!*

She let herself cry, but mostly she just sat and thought
. . . about love and failure and, she went bravely on, the
possibility of healing.

She had no idea how long she'd been sitting there when
she sensed a presence in the darkness. Her eyes were so
glazed with tears, she could barely see. Alarmed, she cried
out hoarsely, *"Who's out there?!"*

A sound of crunching leaves and of somebody's throat
being cleared. Then she saw the faint bobbing of a small,
low-powered flashlight coming her way.

"Oh, I'm sorry, Mrs. Rafferty. I didn't see you sitting
there. I've just been, uh, walking about the place. It got
dark while I was unpacking, and it turns out none of the
lamps in the cottage have any bulbs in them. I hate to
bother you, but I believe there are some stored in that util-
ity cabinet in the kitchen."

When he got to the porch steps, she knew he could tell
that she'd been crying. But there seemed to be something
kind of funny and guarded about his face, too. His eyes
were sort of bleary; his voice had sounded raw.

"Light bulbs?"

"Yeah. I think there's a bunch of them in that cabinet
near the back door."

"Of course. I'll check."

"I've been, uh, down by the pond. . . ."

"That can't have been easy."

"It's the first time I've been there since— I'm sorry, you
don't need to hear this just now, do you?"

"Let me get you those light bulbs. I'll be right out."

In the kitchen, she hurriedly wiped her face, took an ice
cube out of the refrigerator, wrapped it in a napkin, and
pressed it to her eyes and cheeks. Then she went to the
cabinet and took out a corrugated package that contained
half a dozen sixty-watt bulbs. As she neared the partially
open screen door, she could see that he'd sat down on the
steps. His head was in his hands and his shoulders were
moving up and down.

106

She stood there a minute, and then began to move more forcefully, her footsteps echoing on the wooden floor, to give him a chance to compose himself. When she stepped out and handed the package to him, he had recovered enough to say, "Thank you. These should certainly last me awhile, shouldn't they?" His uneven grin betrayed effort.

He put the bulbs on the step beneath him and remained seated. Madeleine sat down next to him. They just sat there quietly listening to the crickets, looking out at the dark. Then he stood up to go. As he stooped to pick up the package of bulbs, he reached over and patted her hand. And then—perhaps accidentally—this became a brief caress. A warm, kind, deliberate stroke that left a lingering sensation on her hand.

"Good night, Madeleine. Things usually look better in the morning."

"Good night, Harry. Hope you're right."

And then he was gone. The dark just swallowed him up. Madeleine remained seated on the steps for a while. Then she thought of something that, in spite of everything, made her face break into a smile. It was the lovely line from *Henry V:* "A little touch of Harry in the night."

Still smiling over the line's unlikely aptness, and having received a curiously parallel infusion of courage from its recollection, she stood up to go inside. As she went to turn off the light by the front door, she caught sight of Missie's bulging laundry case. She picked it up and tossed it carelessly inside the doorway. Then she locked up for the night and went to sleep.

Back in his cabin, Harry busied himself putting in the light bulbs. The cozy normalcy of their soft light in that small space had a calming effect. He finished unpacking his few belongings and settled in. He climbed into bed, remembering something he'd seen in Madeleine Rafferty's face, wondering about it. The thought that sent him sliding effortlessly into a deep, restorative night's sleep was "Whatever else she's going through, the lady sure does love this place."

By the time Harry Littlefield finished unpacking and moving into his guest cottage up in Indian Meadow, Gilbert Rafferty—down at his studio on West Twenty-sixth Street in New York City—was just finishing the last of his moving out. As he would be leaving behind a goodly number of belligerent creditors, he prepared his farewell message with particular care. The phone wouldn't be turned off for another month.

"Hello, this is Gilbert Rafferty speaking. I am out of town on assignment at present and shall be away from the studio for some time." He'd recorded a prior version that had said "for an indefinite period," but "some time" sounded better. More positive. "At the tone, please leave your name and number, and I will get back to you . . . eventually." Then he recorded it again, leaving off the "eventually."

He played this version over again, listening with satisfaction to the smooth, professional sound of his voice. He played it back several times. That person speaking was the person he liked to think he was.

At last he glanced around the desolate studio to see if he'd forgotten anything. All of his heavy photographic equipment was gone. Sold at a loss. The space was empty. Except for some black-and-white blowups still displayed on the wall, there was nothing left. An especially arresting portrait he'd taken of Elizabeth and Matilda some years back caught his eye. One of his best. Maybe he'd take 'em out to L.A. . . . . get into the video scene. That's where the real money was.

His green travertine obelisk, now noticeably chipped along one side, stood on the otherwise empty desk. Obeying some vagrant, unfocused impulse, he decided to pack that, too. He tucked it in gently among the small plastic baggies full of white powder purchased with the proceeds of the sale of his equipment.

He'd get an early start in the morning.

CHAPTER

12

ON Saturdays, in order to get a decent head start on their busiest day of the week, Joe Mitford would often fix breakfast an hour early. By six-thirty that morning, he'd prepared scrambled eggs and bacon and was just taking some piping-hot Freihofer's blueberry muffins out of the toaster oven when his mother entered the kitchen. She was dressed for work in a bright salmon-colored pantsuit, which she'd accessorized with a pair of large square plastic earrings in the exact same shade. Her makeup—a rosy-hued layer of liquid base, lots of pink blush, turquoise eyeshadow, and carefully layered brown mascara—had already been applied for the day. Except for lipstick, the final touch. She would put that on after breakfast, on their way out, at the ormolu mirror above the hall table. This routine rarely varied.

They ate in companionable silence, reading the local paper, scrupulously checking each and every real estate listing. Theirs and their competitors.

At seven, Mrs. Mitford poured herself a second cup of

coffee, and said, "So. Miss High and Mighty won't be joining us today, either, I take it? And what's her excuse this time, I'd like to know? Nor has she offered even once to spell you with the cooking, or clean up afterward, or God forbid, contribute one penny toward her keep."

Well might Mrs. Mitford complain. She missed their old routine. Joe cooked breakfast; she cooked dinner. They took turns with the marketing. Everything smooth and predictable, the way she liked it.

"Ever since that child reappeared on my doorstep, things have been upside-down around here. She made her choice twenty years ago. Running away to California. Not the first time she ran away, either, was it? Who would have thought she'd want to come all the way back here after all that time? And she's as addled as ever; no use to us or anyone else."

"Oh, Joseph, I don't know. I wish I'd understood more about . . . well, you're certainly old enough to hear this now I suppose. . . . When I was a young woman, nobody told me how to go about . . . well, preventing babies, you know. Six! Two of them years after I ought to have stopped. I don't think God himself could have wanted to put me through those last two pregnancies. Full of problems—and look at what they produced. Nothing but more problems. Melissa, so addled, so, well, *puny*. And of course you, my dear boy, the last—born to me in my thirty-eighth year. Your terrible affliction. God knows, I've tried to bear the pain. But honestly, I think to this day, there just wasn't enough left inside of me to produce any more children. My womb had simply worn out." This conversation, or one very like it, had itself become an obligatory routine ever since Pamela Perry Mitford's youngest and frailest daughter, forty-four-year-old Missie Mitford Rollins, had ignominiously returned to her mother's house in tears nearly two months before.

But this morning, Joe's reply would not be routine.

"Mother . . . about Missie . . . ."

110

"Umm?" She'd just bitten off another piece of warm, buttery blueberry muffin.

Joe paused, considering how best to phrase this. "She's more than addled. I think she's sick. In her head."

"Joseph! You can't mean it. After all, she *is* a Mitford. *And* a Perry, on my side." Mrs. Mitford's tone was a mild "tut-tut." She took another bite of muffin, chewing thoughtfully. "Now, mind you, I'll be the first to admit that she's always been something of a problem child. But she does have her good points. She does try. And she has such nice manners, don't you think, once she's up and around? Such a nice way with clients. . . ."

"Mother. Do you know why she's always so late getting up, why she's so sleepy all the time?"

"Takes after her father's side of the family. His sister Isabelle—Aunt Belle, remember?—lacked energy. They were always carting her off to some new doctor or other, trying some new regimen—pills, tonics, I don't know what all."

Joe bit the bullet. He had to tell her. It was going to be one hell of a scene.

"Mother, the reason Missie's always so tired is that she goes out every night. Every night, Mother. Once we've gone to bed, she slips out the back door."

"Joseph! You don't mean it! How can you say such a thing? Missie? Little Missie? Wherever would she go?" A crimson flush appeared beneath Mrs. Mitford's careful layers of makeup.

"I know where she goes. I've followed her."

Their conversation went downhill rapidly after that, as he knew it would. And then, abruptly, she turned the brunt of her considerable ire onto him. Calling his judgment into question, making Missie sound like a dear, delicate creature, so artistic and misunderstood.

"She hasn't had an easy time of it, has she? Poor thing. Married to that pond-scummy Roger Rollins. All he put her through . . . well, the less said about that the better. I don't know why you want to make such a fuss about this, Joseph. She's your *sister,* after all. Why don't you give her a chance to settle in? She's bound to snap out of it. What possible harm can there be in that?"

Joe told her.

"So you see, I've really got to tell the constable, Mother. Somebody's life could be at stake."

"I don't believe it. Not for a minute. I think *you've* gone a bit sick in the head, if you want my honest opinion." But this was said without her usual force. Her voice had become wheedling, quavery. And for a moment, Joe could see the seventy-seven-year-old woman who resided behind that artfully maintained facade of indeterminate middle-age. "Joe . . . couldn't you hold off on this? We've got such a busy day ahead of us—all those folks coming up from New York and that couple from Hartford, and I don't know what all—I'm going to need you there every minute, son. Please? Surely this can keep till Monday. Constable Wilbur probably won't be around until then, anyway." Maybe Joe would just forget about the whole thing. Maybe they could just go on as though nothing had happened. Maybe Missie would just decide to go back to California and leave them in peace!

"Okay, Mother," Joe said. "I guess it can keep until then."

Constable Wilbur—as both Mitfords ought to have known—always came in on Saturdays. It tended to be one of his busiest days, as well. And if there happened not to be any "new business," this was the day he liked to use to put things in order—reading reports, taking care of paper-work. When he came in at eight-thirty that morning, Madeleine Rafferty's three o'clock appointment to discuss her prowler was the only thing actually written down in his notebook.

A prowler. An intruder of some kind. Toys taken from the toy barn. He, Tim Welch, and the men from the sher-

112

iff's office had searched that big, cluttered space every which way and had found nothing, absolutely nothing. But who was to say that there mightn't have been something of importance they hadn't recognized? After all, with such a confusing conglomeration of objects arranged in no particular order, how could they have spotted something missing or out of place?

Could Hillary Littlefield have met this alleged intruder in the toy barn? Might there have been a confrontation? Well, best not get too much ahead of himself.

The day had begun mild and slightly overcast, but toward noon the cloud cover darkened and thickened. Breakfast at the Perry house that morning had been very late and very leisurely. They all just sat around talking and laughing. Rose imitated Tillie's unique technique of climbing, demonstrating how closely it resembled a dance she had done in the long-ago days of her youth. "It was called the Monkey," she recalled. And for a time, both she and Madeleine were transported back to the past, remembering one silly dance step after another—the Mashed Potato, the Frug, and so on—until they were all laughing so hard tears were streaming down their faces.

"Sheesh! Why do grown-ups get so silly, sometimes?" Libby who'd been laughing right along with them, was nevertheless embarrassed by their temporary loss of dignity. But Tillie was intrigued. After all, wasn't it her own recently established prowess as a climber of mountains that had inspired all this?

By the time Madeleine and Rose had cleared away the breakfast dishes, a fine steady drizzle had begun. Libby and Tillie played on the porch until the drizzle became angled and needle-sharp, cutting across the field toward the house, slickening the surface of everything on the porch. They headed inside.

They entered the front door, slamming it behind them,

113

and tripped over the oxblood-colored suitcase Madeleine had thrown carelessly into the hallway the night before.

Half an hour later, Rose, who'd been on her way upstairs to get a sweater, found the two of them sitting there on the floor, the suitcase opened, and the notebooks scattered and piled up every which way between them. They were deep into a game.

Curious, Rose kneeled down alongside them, picking up a book, leafing through the ruled pages at random.

"Madeleine, come take a look!" The pages were completely covered in script. She noticed that the left-hand pages were all upside-down and followed in sequence from the back cover, like books in Hebrew. The right-hand pages began at the front of the book and followed through that way to the end. One side was written in a tight, smeary heavily pressured hand, while the other was loose, loopy, and schoolgirlish, the *I*'s dotted like little circles.

Madeleine stepped into the hallway, and Rose said, "Will you look at these weird notebooks? Where did they come from, anyway?"

"Oh, Lord, I forgot I left that there. Girls, I'm afraid you'd better not play with those. They don't belong to us. Somebody gave them to me to look over, and I haven't had the time to. Better put all of those notebooks back into the suitcase for now, okay?" She scooped the books up and placed them back in the case, shaking her head in embarrassment at her involvement, however reluctant, in anything so obviously crazy and bizarre.

"Aww, we were playing a real good game!"

"We weren't hurting them any. Couldn't we play some more? I promise we won't mess them up."

"I'm sorry, kids, but no. They belong to somebody who thinks they're very important. We can't use them to play with. I'm going to put them away in my closet. I'll deal with them later. Maybe." She said the last word directly to Rose, and they exchanged a look. She mouthed the name Missie Rollins above the children's heads. Rose nodded.

"I might have guessed!" Rose said aloud. "Wait till you see, Madeleine," she continued, following Madeleine into her room as she took the case to her closet. "She's got two completely different handwritings in there. What d'you think that means?"

"No kidding? Say, maybe I will look these over later, after all. Maybe she's just nutty enough to be of, um, some kind of clinical interest."

"How'd you get this stuff, anyway?"

Madeleine explained.

Rose grinned. "She thinks there's a great novel in there, eh?"

"It happens all the time, Rose, in the glamorous world of publishing."

Madeleine decided she'd drive into town early and get some research in at the library before meeting the constable at the firehouse. It was raining steadily. The ground had already become thoroughly saturated, and there were large puddles on the road to Indian Meadow.

Now that she had Lena and Phoebe launched on their hazardous cross-country journey by Conestoga wagon, her fuzzy grasp of nineteenth-century history had become a problem. What were the names of the Indian tribes with whom they might come in contact? What were the dates of actual battles—weren't they always called "massacres"?— that took place during the 1850s? Although she didn't expect to find much in that small village library, which was open on Saturdays only from ten o'clock to six, a couple of basic history texts would certainly help. And it would be nice to leaf through old *American Heritage* magazines, if they had any.

She needed to come up with a good name for a settlement where her women would seek refuge. It would be here that they'd meet Ambrose Alcott, the mysterious and ambiguous hero, a handsome stranger making his way to Utah—who was soon to woo them both, each without the other's knowledge. Only when he proposed marriage to both would it be revealed that he was a Mormon. She hoped to find an actual settlement with a catchy, atmospheric name. Her present idea for a title was *Refuge at———*. Or perhaps *No Refuge at———*, depending on her story's conclusion, which was still up in the air. *Refuge at Lonesome Prairie* by Madeleine Rafferty. *No Refuge at Purgatory Rock* by Madeleine Rafferty. Suddenly, she felt as foolish as Missie Rollins. At least she had enough sense to laugh at herself.

Rose took the girls to the toy barn to play. The rain drummed steadily on the old slate roof, and the old-fashioned light fixtures dangling from the big wooden beams bathed the interior with warm light. Libby and Tillie began to play with the dolls located near the center of the barn, not too far from the ladderlike steps to the hayloft. They used the structure of the steps to create a playhouse, hanging doll blankets from the rungs to serve as walls. At first they played with the big baby doll they'd once fought so viciously over, but before long they'd helped themselves to all kinds of dolls, practically emptying the shelves as they kept adding new characters to their game.

Rose, sitting in the old Windsor chair near the door, had taken along the sweater she was knitting for Jake and was enjoying the soothing mindlessness of her task. It was getting to the point where she would need to measure it against his shoulders. God, Jake's shoulders! What she wouldn't give to place this sweater up against them right this minute. What she wouldn't give to place *herself* up against him . . . all of him! It had been six weeks since he'd left for Canada. He could be back any day, now. She missed him so much!

And at that very moment, Jake Charpentier opened the big barn doors, approaching Rose from behind. He wrapped his strong muscled arms around her—unfinished sweater, knitting needles, and all. At first she thought the sheer force of her longing must have triggered a sense

116

memory that was so powerful and so specific in its particulars as to make its object seem actually to have materialized.

And then of course she knew. This was no apparition. This was Jake, her beloved, come home!

And, oh, he felt good to her. Their subsequent kissing and embracing was frantic, unrestrained, unbuttoned, unzipped. It felt as though their bodies were trying to do everything, then and there, that they ever remembered having done together in the past. A small part of what was left of Rose's mind rejoiced in the knowledge that Libby and Tillie were around the corner, hidden from view.

"How'd you know to find me here?" she whispered.

"But don't you remember? You sent word you'd be staying in the toy barn," he whispered back, without knowing why. "I didn't know if I'd find you here now, but I thought maybe since it's raining, it was worth a try. And I was right, wasn't I? Eh? Was I right? Do I feel right to you? Hmm? And this, does this feel right, too? Eh?"

He was mumbling huskily into her chest, his voice muffled by her lovely naked breasts. She kept her voice quiet and, covering herself up as she spoke, quickly explained the situation to him. Especially about the two little girls right there in the barn with them. His response was to lift her out of her chair, let the knitting fall to the floor, and steal away with her on tiptoe.

"You must let me take you away from all this, my dear," he said, his left eyebrow raised in a stagy, seductive way, his beautiful white teeth flashing in a wicked grin. Just as they got to the door, Rose stopped. She cleared her throat and, modestly holding together her opened shirt, called out to Libby and Tillie, who could not see her in any case, and had apparently not heard or paid the slightest attention to Jake's entrance.

"Ahem. Libby? Tillie? I'm going outside for a bit. Okay? I'll be, um, right back."

"Okay. See ya later."

"Okay. G'bye. Hey, no fair, Libby. That one was mine! You promised! Gimme her back."

The next thing Rose knew, she and Jake were outside, half undressed, scampering in the chill rain. She protested, a bit feebly, that she was worried about leaving her two little charges behind unsupervised. Jake shrugged this off.

"What can possibly happen?" he said. "We'll be right out here. Come. Come see our beautiful new van. I parked it real close to show you."

And the van was beautiful. Shiny metallic-blue paint, gleaming chrome wheel covers, smoked-glass windows, and a sumptuous light blue custom interior that was so plush it simply demanded to be put to urgent, concerted use.

CHAPTER

13

WHEN you opened the little suitcase that came with the Shirley Temple doll, it looked just like a tiny closet: teensy little hangers on a rod, drawers that pulled out, everything. And it was full of clothes! Fluttery, old-fashioned dresses with little lace slips attached to them, coats with hats to match, little leather shoes with straps that actually buttoned open and closed.

Libby and Tillie spent quite some time dressing all the other dolls in Shirley Temple clothes. They were perfectly content to ignore the fact that these clothes rarely fit as intended. They were dressing the dolls for the first day of boarding school, a term neither of them quite understood. Libby had read some of the dusty old books in the cupboards up in their room, and one of them had been called *Flossie at Boarding School*. The headmistress in that story, a Mrs. Upton, had been really wicked.

Libby, playing the role of Flossie, walked the curly-haired Shirley Temple doll through her paces. Tillie got to be Mrs. Upton; her doll was a chubby baby with a big china head. They'd managed to stretch one of Shirley Temple's flowing navy-blue coats on the doll like a tightly fitted jacket, and then they tucked a stray scrap of cloth all around underneath. When an examination of every tiny drawer and nook and cranny in the suitcase failed to uncover so much as a single safety pin, they simply fastened Mrs. Upton's improvised skirt with one of Tillie's barettes. It looked fine.

They paid no attention to the neat, four-by-five-inch brushed stainless-steel container their rummaging had unearthed at the bottom of the suitcase. It was just an ordinary micro-casette recorder. While it didn't have any bearing on their game, its being there among the doll things didn't strike them as unusual—or anachronistic.

They went on to distribute the roles of the rest of the characters in the story—Nellie, Opal, Pansy, and Daisy—between them. This game and its intricate boarding school setting, wedged in among the steps to the hayloft, had all the earmarks of one that would continue for days and days. It felt real.

They never heard Jake's arrival.

They barely noted Rose's departure.

And when, some minutes later, Missie Rollins quietly slipped through the partially opened doors, they took no notice of that, either.

They had no idea they weren't absolutely alone, attending school at this skewed, mythical, thoroughly compelling place they'd conjured up out of their parallel imaginations.

And then all of a sudden this skinny big kid in a weird pink dress came up to Libby from out of nowhere and asked if she could play. Libby and Tillie looked at each other dubiously, shrugging their shoulders.

"We're playing Boarding School. Do you know how to play that?"

"Ooh, yes, I do. That's one of my favorites!"

Libby didn't know about this kid. For one thing, she looked too big to be playing with them. She had all this

120

long crinkly blond hair hanging down her back and a pink ribbon across the top of her head like Alice in Wonderland or something, and personally she gave Libby the creeps.

Tillie, younger and not quite as observant as her sister, simply saw somebody she could boss around.

"Here, you take these two dolls and you be Pansy and Daisy. You have to do what I say. I'm Mrs. Upton, the wicked headmistress."

"Oooh, goody, you're playing *Flossie at Boarding School,* aren't you? That's such a good book—I've read it simply hundreds of times!"

"Oh, yeah?" Libby said. "Really a hundred times? C'mon, you expect me to believe that? I've only read it once, and I think that's quite enough. It's kind of a silly book. Look, if you really want to play with us, you'll just have to do what we say and not get in the way, okay? What's your name?"

"Missie. Missie Mitford. And I bet you don't even know how to *count* all the way to a hundred, so there."

"I can, too," Libby replied defensively, and left it at that. "Okay, these are your two dolls. Mrs. Upton is showing us to our rooms now."

For a while they went on playing as before. It was okay, Libby supposed, but it wasn't the same. She was becoming annoyed. This girl was a total dork. She talked funny. And she kept getting up and bopping around all over the place, picking up toys that had nothing to do with their game and saying they should play with them. Libby decided she didn't like Missie very much and didn't want to play with her anymore.

"Missie, we can't play with you anymore. Go on home, now, okay?"

Missie began to cry. "Oh, no! Please! Please let me stay a little while longer. If I go home my sisters will pick on me. They're mean and awful and I hate them. I promise I'll play just the way you want me to . . . please!"

"We were having a lot more fun before you got here."

121

"Wait! I know what let's do! Something really fun. I can show you a secret! My family comes here every summer, you know, and I know a secret about this place nobody else knows. Last year? My mother made my big sisters play with me in here one day. That's when they showed it to me. They swore me to secrecy, of course. Made me sign an oath in blood. I've never breathed a word to a soul! But I'll show it to you because I want so much for us to be friends. Would you like to see it? You'll have to promise not to tell."

"What's that supposed to mean, 'sign an oath in blood'?" Libby asked, sounding cynical and suspicious. But she felt a quickening rush of dangerous curiosity. A secret. Something even grown-ups didn't know.

Missie reached over to them, taking each by the hand.

"It's just around the corner from where we're standing now, but you'd never know to look at it! Come along, I'll show you. Nobody else in the whole world knows about this."

"Except your sisters."

"Oh, them. Well, yes."

They were now standing behind the open stairs to the loft. The wooden planking at the base had a couple of large cardboard boxes on it filled with bits and pieces of broken toys. Missie pushed these away with both hands, really putting her back into it, because they were quite heavy. And when she was done, she kicked one with her foot for good measure. Libby noticed her dorky shoes: ungainly yellow-ish sandals that exposed her long and ugly toes. Now Missie bent down and put her fingers through a knot hole in the wide center board. Libby and Tillie stood back, a bit scared, watching intently.

She lifted up this board like the lid to a box. There was a hook on the back of one of the stair rungs, and by inserting this through the knot hole, Missie was able to secure it in an opened position.

"Now the fun begins, girls. Follow me!"

122

The entrance was quite small and very dark. Tillie didn't like the look of it. Libby, still thrilling to a sense of secret and forbidden knowledge, was thinking that probably the reason why no grown-ups knew about this was that the opening was much too small for most of the grown-ups she knew.

Missie, who had to be at least twelve, had to step sideways and suck her gut in. But she led the way, as Libby and then Tillie stepped down after her. There were rough stone steps leading straight down. A large square flashlight hung from the wall by a strap. Missie took it down, turned it on, and slung the strap over her arm like a purse, keeping her hands free. The steps turned a corner and went down some more.

"I don't like this," Tillie said. "I'm going back up."

"But, wait, I haven't even shown you the surprise yet!"

"I don't *care*! It's dark and damp and creepy down here, and I don't like it one bit. I'm going back up."

In a flash, Missie had pushed past Libby and was lunging fiercely at Tillie, grabbing her roughly by the wrist.

"You're coming with me, young lady. And you're not going back up until I'm good and ready to *let* you go back up. Now is that clear?" She grabbed hold of Libby's wrist with her other hand and dragged them both down, bumpity-bump on their fannies, until they reached the bottom step. They were in some kind of storeroom with a packed earthen floor and the huge rough boulders of the barn's foundation looming up all around them in a cavelike arch. The flashlight threw weak, jittery bands of light zigging and zagging up and down the walls. Missie shifted the strap to her hand and beamed the light straight ahead.

"It's just up ahead, girls. Wait till you see, you'll just love it." She said this calm as you please in her old voice, as though she'd never pushed or shoved them, or yelled at them, or frightened them at all.

She put her hands on Tillie and Libby's backs and prodded them firmly forward. They both jumped, afraid something more violent would follow. The moment Libby felt the touch of that hand on her back, she understood what had until then been only a fuzzy unfocused suspicion.

This Missie was no kid. She was some kind of crazy grown-up! It was this realization that finally prompted her to rebel.

Glancing instinctively over her shoulder, Libby pulled away from the woman's touch in disgust. Missie moved forward to regain her hand's contact with Libby's recalcitrant back. As she did so, the flashlight's beam illuminated her face from below, turning it into a grotesque mask.

"You're no kid!" Libby yelled. "You're nothing but a crazy grown-up. And you'd better let us go, or I'm telling!"

"Oh, no you don't!" Missie shouted back. "You think you can get me in trouble like you did last year, don't you? Well, this time it's not going to work. This time, I'm bigger than both of you and smarter, too. And this time you're not getting away with it, so there!" She threw the flashlight down at them with all her might. It didn't hit either Libby or Tillie, but it scared and distracted them. And during that object's brief, clattering fall to the ground, Missie had begun speeding back up the steps.

By the time the girls had recovered enough to retrieve the still-functioning flashlight and began tripping all over themselves in an anxious, uncoordinated effort to mount the steep, uneven stone steps, Missie had reached the top. They were just able to hear her breathless, wheezing cackle of triumph as she let the heavy wooden board drop down with a crashing thud.

The impact caused a shower of crumbling dirt to rain down upon Libby and Tillie's upturned faces as they huddled near the top. Then they heard the dull scraping sound of first one and then the other cardboard carton being shoved back into place.

The Indian Meadow Free Library surprised Madeleine with a far better than adequate collection of books on nine-

124

teenth-century American history. It was situated, alas, in the reference section, a small rarely used room located in the basement. Madeleine guessed it once must have served as the scullery of the old Victorian house some benefactor had donated to the village. So there she sat, at a table that was noticeably too high for her, on a chair that wobbled and creaked, squinting to decipher small print on yellowish old paper. She noted down such facts and local color as might be useful to her story and, despite the discomforts of her situation, had become so absorbed by the task as to almost forget her meeting with the constable.

A clock somewhere upstairs struck the hour of three, and she sat up with a start. She'd have to come back to this. She neatly lined up the books she'd been using on the table and left her legal pad and pen there next to them.

It was just a two-block walk to the firehouse—as indeed it would have been to any destination in that small village—so Madeleine left her car parked where it was, first stopping to take an umbrella out of the trunk. It was raining hard and steadily. The sky was so dark that the few streetlights had come on.

When she arrived, she found the constable's office door closed and heard raised, angry voices coming from inside. She took a seat.

It had turned out to be a day full of "new business" for Emmett Wilbur. A break-in and burglary at a gas station out near the Northway. A violent domestic disturbance between a vacationing couple that had turned rather dangerous. Nothing like a rainy, claustrophobic Saturday in a leaking tent to bring old resentments to a boil. And now this: poor Mrs. Congdon, who attended his wife Harriet's church, in with her son Sean. He'd been in a fight—bloody face, swollen nose, defiant glare flashing first at his mother, then at the constable.

"I can't do anything with him, Mr. Wilbur! He's in with that bunch of hooligans—motorcycle dopers, all of them. What they want with him, I can't imagine. He's barely fifteen! He won't even tell me what the fight was about. I just can't control him anymore. Couldn't you talk some sense into him for me? I swear he's fixing to turn out bad, just like his brother.

And his father before him, she might have added. Mr. Congdon had been away doing time for armed robbery during Wilbur's entire tenure here in Indian Meadow. He considered holding the boy on some kind of juvenile drunk and disorderly charge, but there was no real cause. Nobody had lodged a complaint against him. The kid needed a male authority figure, and the conscientious constable decided to try to fill the bill. He asked Sean's mother to step outside.

Mrs. Congdon came out and sat down next to Madeleine, who wondered how long she might have to wait, and wished she'd thought to bring some work along.

The yelling and cursing and screaming provoked by Emmett Wilbur's good intentions were loud enough for both women to hear. Every word.

The sound of that raw, husky voice—still poignantly inclined to squeak like a rusty gate without warning—assaulted Madeleine's ears. She found this sudden, unexpected exposure to the heat of this unseen boy's brute emotions physically upsetting. She wished she hadn't agreed to come down here today. She didn't need this. Her own emotions weren't all that steady to begin with.

"I can't control him anymore!" the woman beside her sobbed. "He won't listen to anyone! Ah, dear God, he's lost to me . . . I've lost him for sure!" Inside, the boy's tirade reached a crescendo.

"You ain't got diddly squat on me, asshole, so why don't you just fuck off, okay? Why don't you just take this whole goddamn shitty town and shove it. I'm *outa* here!"

When Wilbur at last ushered Madeleine into his office, he apologized for the unfortunate disturbance and offered her a cup of coffee, which she accepted gratefully.

"I sometimes wonder how anybody manages to get along with anybody anymore," she said, sipping the strong, excel-

126

lent coffee from a plastic foam cup. "That poor woman! I felt so sorry for her. Was that boy this year's version of Jake Charpentier?"

"Ah, no, young Sean's much worse. Can't say I hold out much hope for him. It's true Jake was often in trouble— although most of all that happened before I came here. Still and all, Jake always had a kind of charm about him. In spite of his hotheadedness, he was always—oh—well-spoken, I guess you'd have to call it.

"Well, enough of that. Now, I wish you'd tell me everything you can remember about this intruder. How many separate incidents there may have been . . . all that."

It only took a few minutes. Then she was out on her own again with plenty of time still to spare for the library. Nineteenth-century frontier life—despite its many obvious and well-recorded dangers—seemed to offer a comforting respite from the present.

Jake Charpentier and Rose Bedard, arms entwined, smiled softly at each other in relaxed, post-coital languor.

"My God, Jake, but I've missed you!"

"It's great to be back, kid." He kissed her nose.

She laughed and began to sit up slowly, stretching her arms luxuriously above her head. "I'd better go, though. Got to get back to the kids. Want to come along? Let me introduce you to Libby and Tillie. I've told them all about you!"

"Oh, yeah? Like what?"

"Oh, how good-looking you are. How, um, well-hung you are, things like that."

"You did, eh? Is nothing sacred?" He threw the shirt she'd been wearing at her, and, catching it, she began somewhat reluctantly to put it back on.

They ran back to the barn through the rain. Jake had parked his big new van so close that it was just a few steps.

"Libby! Tillie! C'm'here! I've got somebody here wants to meet you. Libby? Tillie?"

127

Rose walked in, past the abandoned dolls, over to the blanket-draped ladder to the loft. The open Shirley Temple suitcase sat where it had been abandoned on the bottom rung.

Rose began running in and out among the tall glass-fronted cabinets. Again she called, "Libby! Tillie!" She darted up the steps to the small, shallow loft, which was filled, as it had been for as long as she could remember, with battered canvas canoes, collapsed inflatable rafts, and dusty crates and bundles. Undisturbed. Nobody'd been up here in decades.

Holding on to the rung above her for support, she was able to lean out and look down on virtually the entire barn. Libby and Tillie were not to be seen anywhere.

"Libby, Tillie? Come out, come out wherever you are! Front and center. *Now*. This is for real. I'm not joking!"

Nothing. Nobody. Eerie silence. Jake, who was still standing by the big doors, looked up at her. Baffled, her heart beginning to sound an alarm, Rose said, "Jake? They don't seem to be here!"

CHAPTER

14

WHEN Gilbert Rafferty and his fifteen-year-old BMW 2002 TII had both been young and full of promise, he'd fancied that its gleaming paint was the same color as a kind of sparkling orangeade he'd enjoyed at sidewalk cafés along the French Riviera during his junior year abroad. And even now it seemed to him the jaunty auto wore its long and picaresque history of misadventure on city streets with a kind of rakish insouciance. It was still a car to reckon with. Especially on the open road.

This ride up the New York State Thruway was just the ticket. Although the day was overcast, the highway afforded more than its share of broad, inspiring vistas. He pulled over into the same lookout Madeleine and Libby and Tillie had stopped at nearly a month before. Minolta in hand, he surveyed the scene, trying to frame it with one of the craggy rock formations that had been dynamited into existence by road crews many years before. He felt challenged by the novelty of shooting something purely scenic. Somehow this seemed to demand black-and-white film.

Soft, shimmery grays; deep, velvety blacks; infinite; enduring. Edward Weston. Ansel Adams. That sort of thing. He fussed contentedly with his equipment for a time, employing several filters and wide-angle lenses, and ended up shooting an entire roll of Kodak Panatomic X film.

Satisfied, he returned to the BMW and resumed his journey. The more distance he put between himself and New York City, the better he began to feel. For a time he toyed with the possibility that, rather than merely escaping from the tacky disappointments of his past life, he was in fact driving toward a new beginning. A fresh start! A reconciliation! Maybe, at some time in the future, he would look back fondly on this day: the day his life finally turned around.

His threadbare and inconstant mind conjured up an imaginary snapshot of Libby and Tillie and Maddie posing in front of some gabled cottage. And, yes, there he was, the husband and father, walking toward them up a pretty flagstone path! Then the snapshot dissipated, tearing itself up into small sharp-edged bits somewhere behind his eyes. There were sharp, angry zaps of pain behind his eyes.

He would stop at the next rest stop and do a couple of lines.

Spitting yucky, crumbly dirt out of their mouths and wiping their tearing eyes and smudged faces, Libby and Tillie retreated from the entrance. The fine steady stream of silty small pebbles continued to pursue them down the steps, but now fell more or less innocuously upon their necks and down their backs.

Libby held the flashlight, peering into the narrow passage ahead.

"What do you think is in there?"

"She was going to show us a surprise."

Neither had the sense that their situation was anything but temporary—soon to be put comfortably to rights by some grown-up.

The passageway, so narrow as to require them to walk single file, sloped slightly downhill. The walls were a combination of packed dirt and cobble, and the ceiling became progressively lower as they went along. Tillie was the first to see the crude arrow scratched on the wall.

"Look, a sign!"

"It's like on the subway—follow the arrows to the shuttle."

They continued for quite some distance until the passage had virtually become a crawl space. They were small enough to be able to walk upright. Another arrow. And above it, a word, scratched in primitive, unschooled letters.

"F R e e D u m," it said. A little farther along, two more words appeared: "p R A i Z G o D."

Now there was a widening in the space, and for the first time both girls became really afraid. At last they realized that this was serious, that this might be for keeps. Because beyond this widening, this dungeonlike partial oblong of a room defined by thick, rough-hewn timbers, there was nothing more—nothing at all.

The passage did not continue. The far wall of this chamber might indeed have once provided a way out, but it was there no longer. Now, a ceiling-high jumble of drippy, muddy debris, gravel, stones, rocks, and great big tumbled-in boulders closed off all possibility of access.

"We'll just have to go back." Libby announced with an effort at nonchalance. But Tillie detected the tremble in her sister's voice.

"Do you think we can open up that lid?"

"Maybe if we both push real hard."

The walk back seemed interminable. At last the passageway grew broader, the ceiling became noticeably higher, and the ground appeared to be heading uphill once more.

Then there were the steps, flickering unpleasantly in the flashlight's faint beam. They mounted them. Libby hung the flashlight back on its hook and tried to shove the heavy wooden board that blocked the entrance. Tillie joined her. Both gave a great heave. "Unghh!" A new rain of dust and silt was let loose, but the board gave no sign of budging. They tried again. And again.

"Maybe we could yell? Maybe somebody in the barn will hear us!"

"Rose! Mommy! Help!"

They shouted until their voices cracked, banging the board with their fists until their knuckles were scraped sore. Debris, falling continuously into their faces from above, added torturously to their overall discomfort. Yet they kept shouting and banging for what seemed like hours to them. Perhaps ten or twelve minutes.

"Nobody hears us, Tillie. Might as well stop."

"What do we do now?"

"Well, let's don't just sit here feeling sorry for ourselves. Let's go back to the other end. Maybe we missed something. Maybe there's a way out. Remember what the sign said?"

"I couldn't figure out what it said."

"'Freedom.' Don't you know what that means? Like, you know, when you say 'home free all' or 'ally ally oxen free'?"

"You mean that Missie person is playing hide-and-seek with us?"

"Yeah. Maybe. Something like that." Libby didn't believe this, but she figured it would help if Tillie did. "So let's go back to the other end and see if we can't find a way out of here. I bet we can if we try." Libby had unconsciously begun to imitate their mother, who, whenever things got rough, began to talk in a certain tone of voice and say certain kinds of things that always made them feel everything would turn out fine.

Once again they covered the considerable distance to the strange room at the end of the passageway. It was exactly as they had both remembered it, but this time they examined every detail. Especially the mountain of muddy, rocky

132

debris. It was really gross. Slimy mud oozed between scuzzy rocks with green stuff growing on them.

Libby wondered about the moss . . . if that's what it was. Green things need sunlight. She'd learned that in Mr. Sanchez's class last term. So if all green growing things needed sunlight, these rocks had to have been in the sun to get their furry coating. So they probably couldn't have been down here all that long. The rocks must have tumbled in recently. In fact, it looked like there was still some kind of movement going on. A squelching ooze of mud, and within it, a thin trickle of water.

While Libby's mind flexed its nascent powers of deductive reasoning, Tillie's excellent eyes had spotted something down near the base of the rock pile that looked like a scrap of cloth. A triangle of thick, wet gray wool. She gave it a tug. There seemed to be lots more to it. She tugged some more. It pulled out slowly. Tillie really had to work at it, bracing her sturdy feet far apart, rearing way back, using both hands to pull just as hard as she could.

When she'd pulled out some twelve or fourteen inches, an object that had apparently been caught up in the fabric tumbled out. It was a bright red shoe, its high stiletto heel thickly caked with mud. "Look at this, Libby!" Libby came over for a look. She brushed some of the mud off. It was a lovely, elegant high-heeled shoe, and there was some lettering inside it.

"Fer-ra-gamo," Libby read with some difficulty. "It's pretty, isn't it?"

Then the blanket—for that's indeed what it seemed to be—yielded up a spiral notebook, which fell to the ground at Tillie's feet. Libby picked it up. A pen had been nestled inside the wiry spine. "It's like those books in the suitcase!" It appeared that only a few of the pages had been written on. The book was so thoroughly wet, only the faintest traces of ink remained.

By now Tillie had managed to tug out more than two feet of wrinkled, mud-caked cloth. And then Libby heard a sort of low rumble. She sensed a kind of imminence growing and building from deep within.

"Tillie! Stop!" she shouted.

Tillie, whose concentration had been absolute, was startled into letting go of the woolen cloth. She darted backward.

A new mudslide had begun.

Libby lunged toward Tillie, scooping her up by the armpits, flinging her out of the path of the terrifying movement of stone, mud, and water that her innocent tugging had unleashed.

Then it stopped.

The muddy mound of rocks had come forward six to eight feet into the chamber. Hardly any floorspace remained for them. They were sitting in the far corner, huddled in each other's arms, and Tillie was crying out in pain. Her left foot had been hit rather hard by a flying rock. It hurt so much that she almost couldn't stand it. And yet part of her mind still wondered about the blanket she'd nearly pulled free. Where was it now? What other objects might still have come spilling out of it? It was hard to let go of the single-minded connection she'd formed with it.

"I hurt my foot, Libby. It hurts so . . . so . . . *much!* Make it stop, please!"

"I don't know how, Tillie." Helplessly, she looked at her sister's foot. It was swelling up right before their eyes. "Sit over here and keep it up high. I'll wet something in the water to keep it cool." But what? She thought about taking her sweatshirt off, but it was chilly down here, and she wasn't wearing an undershirt.

Libby was wearing long corduroys. She took them off, found a sharp rock, and started a little hole at the knee. Pretty soon she got a good tear going, and pulled off the bottom half of the pants leg. Then, one leg long, the other short, she put her pants back on. She went over to where the water had begun bubbling along like a regular brook. She soaked the scrap of corduroy and brought it over to

Tillie, who laughed in spite of herself at the sight of her sister's funny-looking pants.

Libby wrapped the cold wet scrap of light blue corduroy around Tillie's foot. "I think this will help. Remember when Mommy sprained her ankle? That's what she did. She kept her foot up high on a bunch of pillows and put cold cloths on it."

"That was last Christmas."

"Yeah, she fell on the ice. We were carrying the tree home. Remember?"

"She sure looked funny."

"Yeah." They laughed, remembering. For a moment there, it could have gone either way. They might both as easily have burst into tears.

Rose and Jake searched the toy barn top to bottom, several times. Then they went to the house to see if by any chance the girls might have taken it upon themselves to go there.

"Maybe they had to go to the bathroom."

"Wouldn't you have heard them leave?"

"Jake, all I heard was the blood rushing in my ears."

"Yeah, I guess you're right."

They weren't in the house. Nor was there any sign they had been.

Rose and Jake walked all around the outside of the barn, looking for they didn't know what. They saw nothing unusual. The rough, gravelly path that led to the barn was full of fallen branches and leaves. It was impossible to tell whether anybody other than themselves had used it recently.

"Oh, Jake, what's happened? Where could they have gone off to? Libby and Tillie are two of the most t-t-terrific kids . . ." A wrenching sob came out of her throat without warning.

"Hey, now stop that. We'll find them. Everything's

135

gonna be okay. How far can they have gone in all this rain, anyway?"

"But you don't understand, Jake. That's just the point. They *wouldn't* have gone anywhere! They're smart, good kids. Why on earth would they have left the barn? Oh God, is this going to be Hillary Littlefield all over again?" Now she really began to cry. And Jake heard the story of Hillary Littlefield's death for the first time.

He looked around the area leading to the barn doors. There was nothing to see. Nothing at all. He made up his mind.

"Rose, my love, I think—seeing what you just told me about Mrs. Littlefield—I think maybe we'd better call the constable. If they've somehow disappeared into those woods, we're gonna need help. No point in wasting time trying to find them ourselves. We could mess up."

They phoned Emmett Wilbur from the kitchen. It was nearly four o'clock.

"I'll be right up," he said. "Mrs. Rafferty just left here a short time ago. She should be back there any minute. Wait for me by that barn."

"Anything we can do to help while we're waiting, Constable?" Jake asked.

"Wouldn't hurt to call out their names. Loud as you can. They just might hear you and come running. They could have merely wandered off into the woods, you know. It happens all the time. Be sure to stay put—that way, if they do hear you, they'll have a constant fix."

Rose stood with Jake at the front of the barn, and they began to shout, "Libby! Tillie!" over and over again. Then Rose went into the barn for a while, leaving Jake to continue the job. Her voice had started to break and she couldn't get it to carry.

She crouched down by the steps to the hayloft, picking up one and then another of the toys the girls had so recently been playing with, as though they might provide some hint of how to find them. She smiled wistfully at the

136

eloquence of the little scene they'd left behind, the intensity with which their quirky, lovable personalities still resonated from this odd assemblage of dolls and toys.

"Please, God! Make them be all right! Please, please, please!"

A car was now driving slowly up the driveway through the heavy rain. Contrary to Wilbur's prediction, however, it was not Madeleine's. It was Harry Littlefield's big gray Cherokee. It came to a stop near the main house, and Harry stepped out, pulling up the hood of his waterproof jacket. He heard Jake's anxious, despairing voice shouting "Libby! Tillie!" repeatedly, and without stopping to think, he began running toward the barn.

Jake had been faithfully keeping up his shouting, and Rose felt she ought at least go back outside again and keep him company. Her knees creaking, she made to get up from the crouch she'd held too long and promptly lost her balance. She landed flat on her bottom just where Tillie had sat earlier, wielding the fat Mrs. Upton in her Shirley Temple outfit. Rose got herself clumsily back on her knees, and just as she was about to stand up again, she saw the burnished high-tech gleam of the micro-cassette recorder lying at the bottom of the opened Shirley Temple suitcase. Now, what in the world was that doing there?

"Jake? Jake, come quick. I think I've found something."

When Harry Littlefield reached the door a minute or so later, he was stunned to hear an all-too-well remembered female voice echoing uncannily—and unmistakably!—from within the big old barn. Loud. Bitchy. Slightly nasal.

"Item 122: Shirley Temple doll, eighteen inches tall, circa 1937," it was saying. *"Condition good to excellent."* The sheer impact of memories thus unleashed without warning was enough to buckle his knees. Harry grabbed the doorway for support.

"Item 122a," the late Hillary Littlefield calmly continued, all business, *"Shirley Temple Wardrobe Trunk . . . consisting of . . . hey, don't you know enough to knock? What makes you think you can just barge in like that?"*

137

CHAPTER

15

THE gurgling sound of water coming through the rocks was getting noisier. And there was lots more water on the ground now than there had been before. It was pooling toward them, encroaching their corner. The little room was starting to fill up like a bathtub.

"Tillie," Libby said, "we've got to get out of here right now."

She stood up and walked over to the newly altered formation of rocks and boulders and mud. Her sneakers were wet through. She shone the beam of the flashlight over the whole mess, paying particular attention to the crevices.

Tillie hobbled over to where her sister stood.

"We're gonna have to climb *up*, aren't we . . . see if maybe there's a way to the outside at the top?"

"Uh-huh."

So Tillie, the established climber of rocks, began to scramble upward.

"Sheesh, Tillie, for God's sake! Be careful! You don't want all those rocks falling in on us again."

"I'm being careful, Libby. Besides, my foot hurts too much for me to go fast. Just follow me, okay? Make sure your hands are holding on good and tight, and then step down lightly and, like, *feel* what's under your feet. If it doesn't jiggle or wobble, step down harder. That way you've got time to get away from the bad ones. They're all wet and squishy, but at least they're big, and you can grab hold of the green hairy stuff—it's tough."

"Wait, Tillie, if you're gonna go first, you take the flashlight."

"Nah, I need both hands. You come up behind me with it."

So Libby began to ascend the rockpile, gingerly at first, then gaining in confidence as she followed her younger sister's example.

There was water everywhere. Trickling, spurting, rushing . . . between rocks, from within muddy, sandy crevices . . . it felt as if they were wading uphill. As Tillie climbed, most of the water seemed to be coming in from somewhere high above her right shoulder; she instinctively began moving toward the left. The rocks continued to be just as wet and slippery, but at least she could grab hold of them without groping through several inches of moving water.

Libby was still trying to beam the light up to where Tillie was, holding it first in one hand, and then the other, and finally winding the strap around her arm as she had seen Missie do. But no matter what she did with it, it got in her way. She decided to turn it off to see if they could manage without it. This one moment's distraction cost her her footing and she fell to her knees. She slid two or three feet, and then she stopped, holding on for dear life with both her hands.

"Oh!"

"Oh! Golly! Libby! Are you okay?"

"Shh! Don't move . . . they're gonna tumble again!"

And then poor brave Tillie came crashing awkwardly down toward Libby, her injured foot making her shriek

139

with a lightning-like bolt of pain. Libby somehow managed to grab hold of Tillie's sweatshirt and prevent her from falling farther. They stayed there, wedged together with not an inch to spare between them, tucked into what seemed to be the only ledge to have survived intact while everything around it rumbled terrifyingly downward.

"Oh, God, Libby, what're we gonna do now? My *foot*! I don't think I can even use it."

Libby put her one free arm around Tillie. "Please don't cry, Tillie. We'll get out of this. I promise. Can you, like, shift your weight and maybe sit down here for a minute? I've got to think."

Very, very slowly—any movement might have started another slide—they rearranged themselves on the ledge so that they were both sitting down. Little rocks and pebbles continued to spill down every which way. They heard the ground beneath them give a kind of grunt—a deep, grinding, menacing shift—but it did not travel up to where they were. Libby had lost the flashlight. They could only hear what was happening below them; they could no longer see anything down there.

But wait. Libby could see Tillie perfectly well.

"Tillie! There's light coming in from somewhere!"

They both looked up. There was a small opening, perhaps the size of a basketball, not six feet above their heads. Outdoor forest noises were wafting down from it. And each caught a whiff of fresh, piny outdoor air.

Gilbert Rafferty, starting to wear down from his long and unaccustomed stint behind the wheel, finally began to see occasional roadside references to Indian Meadow. He'd held off lunch, thinking he'd wait until he got there, but now it was after three and he was really hungry, despite the amount of cocaine he had taken.

When at last the jaunty BMW crested the small rise from which the village of Indian Meadow could be seen in its entirety, with Blue Mirror Lake forming its picturesque

140

backdrop, Gil continued on downhill toward it without even realizing he'd arrived. It didn't look like an actual town to him, more like the outskirts to a town.

It had been raining steadily for the last sixty or seventy miles, and a cottony mist was rising from the lake. Ragged patches of fog seemed stuck randomly about the landscape. The hills and mountains beyond the lake were completely obscured. He spotted the Blue Mirror Café with its small graveled parking lot and drove in. He didn't realize he'd arrived in Indian Meadow until he opened up his menu and saw, neatly typed in blurry purple duplicating ink: "Welcome to the Blue Mirror Café, Indian Meadow, New York—Deep in the Heart of the Adirondack Forest."

He ordered a western omelette, complete with a mound of deliciously greasy and oniony home fries. He drank a tall glass of iced tea. He stepped into the men's room and did another line of coke.

By the time he left the café, it was just after four. The air was so fresh up here! He took deep, self-conscious breaths, walking down the street with a silly-ass grin on his face. But for the rain and the guarded condition of his handmade Italian loafers, he might have gone on walking indefinitely, exploring the delights of this quaint out-of-the-way spot. Amazing, you could know a person for more than a dozen years and still be surprised by what they did. He'd had no idea that Madeleine was into this woodsy, outdoorsy stuff. He rather was himself, actually. Maybe they still had a chance of getting back together, after all. He saw the four of them, sitting before a roaring campfire, toasting marshmallows . . . and then realized this picture was one he'd shot on assignment for General Foods some years back. Well. That wasn't the point, was it? The point was that it felt good to be here.

Now . . . how to find where his little family had gone off to? He had no plan. He'd merely located Indian Meadow on a map and had driven straight up. Where would they be? He looked around at the genteel village houses with their careful front yards. Then he saw the big corner building, white clapboard siding, shiny green trim, with the sign that said LAKESHORE REALTY. That should do for a start.

He walked in, and apparently the person in charge had also just arrived. It was a petite, pinched, birdlike woman who was just removing her shiny plastic see-through raincoat. Her plastic, pink polka-dotted umbrella stood open by the doorway, dripping puddles onto the floor. Now she unfastened the see-through plastic kerchief that had been protecting her peculiar hairdo.

"Hello, there!" Gilbert Rafferty said heartily. She straightened up to look at him, and there was something about her attitude and the way the tall-ceilinged, empty shop tilted off somberly behind her that made Gilbert Rafferty think: *Diane Arbus.*

"I'm Missie Rollins," she said wispily, and then by rote, "How may I help you?"

Madeleine pushed the rickety chair away from the high old-fashioned table in the basement reference room and decided she'd done enough for one day. She had a few promising place names, the beginnings of some understanding of how and where travel routes had developed in the first half of the nineteenth century, and a map, which she'd copied, outlining the purview of the major Indian nations. But instead of feeling satisfied with her afternoon's accomplishments, she was headachey and anxious. Her concentration had been so intense that once she let go, it felt as though she'd been cut off from the real world for too long.

Driving through town, she caught an unconscious glimpse of the orange BMW in the parking lot of the Blue Mirror Café. Her mind did not register it. She was intent on getting back up their mountain road just as fast as the steadily lowering shroud of fog, mist, and rain would permit. She was picturing a nice, cozy cup of tea in the kitchen with Rose.

But the next thing Madeleine would get to drink turned out to be a shot of Jack Daniels—just after she'd been informed of Libby and Tillie's disappearance. Harry Littlefield sensed how close she was to fainting, so he rushed to his cottage, grabbed the bourbon and a glass, came running back, poured it out carefully, and gently lifted the glass to Madeleine's mouth, making sure she got it all down.

Madeleine did not faint. She entered into the kind of shock that lets one endure the unendurable. She was pale, her eyes were overly large, but she would not permit herself to consider the worst that could happen. She saw the cars arrive and sat watching silently as a search party was hurriedly organized. There were perhaps twenty people—a dozen friends and neighbors and six volunteer firemen—all under the constable's competent supervision.

The weather wasn't helping. Here it was, one of the longest days of the year, when they might ordinarily have counted on four more hours of daylight, and the visibility was so poor it might as well have been after sunset. Rain, mist, and occasional patches of thick white ground fog effectively obscured much of the mountainside surrounding the Perry place. The heavy moisture in the atmosphere had the further effect of making it hard to tell just exactly where the noises and voices one heard were coming from.

An unusually rainy May and June that year had left the forest thicker and greener than it had ever been, at least in recent memory. The dense undergrowth was as lush as a jungle; everywhere, fat, dripping, succulent leaves were just reaching their peak of growth. Trails were muddy and frequently blocked by large lakelike puddles, making it necessary to scramble up on the verge amid thorny shrubbery and an ensnaring maze of trees. To look down at one's feet in an effort to keep from slipping was to risk a slap in the face by an overhead branch.

There could be no hope of keeping dry. Within minutes jackets, shirts, and pants were soaked through and stout boots were coated beyond recognition in mud as thick and black as tar. But at least it was not cold. It was a warm, clammy seventy degrees. Madeleine was thinking, Even if they're soaked, they'll be all right. We'll get 'em dry and everything will be all right again.

Constable Wilbur was thinking, I'll give this an hour, tops. If we haven't found them by then, I'd best get on the radio and call the troopers in.

Then he joined Tim Welch and Harry Littlefield, and together, not needing to say much about what they were doing, they headed for Little Quaker Pond. Might as well face up to the most horrible possibility first.

As it happened, the sturdy, grubby little hand that was then within inches of grabbing hold of the root that would hoist it to safety, was fully two miles away from Little Quaker Pond.

That is, if you went by land. To a crow it would have been an easy quarter mile. The underground passage permitted a similar directness. Above it, thick forest, steep and rocky terrain, and perhaps most important, the uncharted changeability of the often-flooding creek mandated the slower, more circuitous route.

This stream—a dangerous, raging torrent in the spring that might cease to exist altogether by the end of a dry summer—had always served as an accepted boundary, dividing the Perry land from that of its neighbors. But the last survey done of the area dated from the mid-1950s, and it no longer reflected the stream's course accurately.

When Libby and Tillie at last scrambled to the surface, they were on the stream's left bank. According to the commonly held notion of that terrain, there was no way for anybody to get there. They were cut off from the house by woods that were virtually impenetrable, not to mention a sudden, steep incline that, according to the survey map, would appear to be the site of a hundred-foot waterfall.

There had long been vague rumors of mighty falls hidden deep in those woods, but nobody had ever actually seen them.

Libby and Tillie just lay on the ground in the steady rain

144

for a minute or two, breathing the fresh damp air and grinning at each other. They'd done it! They'd escaped from their underground prison! Now that they were in plain view above ground, surely it would be a simple matter for somebody to find them and get them home.

"Ow! Oh, Libby, my foot is killing me!"

Libby did what she could to make Tillie comfortable, sitting her down on some soft pine needles, elevating her injured foot on a fallen tree trunk.

"I'm so wet! It's cold out here!"

"Tillie, I'm just as wet as you are. It's raining, everything's wet. There's nothing I can do to get you dry. Someone will be along soon, you'll see. I think we should just sit here until we're found." She sat down next to her sister and put an arm around her protectively. She was prepared to wait as long as it took. The climb up that scary slippery wall of loose rocks had just about exhausted her. Now it was up to somebody else.

"Libby?"

"Hmm?"

"When are they gonna come for us?"

"I don't know. Soon, I bet." Libby was so tired, she was almost dozing.

"Libby?"

"Huh?" Libby replied, startled. Tillie's voice sounded all jittery, like her teeth were chattering.

"Libby? You awake?"

"Yeah, sure."

Tillie moved in closer to her. They sat huddled together like that for a time, and then Tillie's shivery little voice piped up again.

"Uh, Libby, could you do me a favor?"

"What?"

"Could you tell me a story, please? Just until they come and find us?"

CHAPTER
16

CONSTABLE Wilbur let himself feel hopeful—at least for the moment. Although the allotted hour was nearly up and the girls had not been found, neither had his worst fear materialized. There had not been two small bodies in the pond.

Everybody had worried that this was going to be "Hillary Littlefield all over again"—and you could certainly understand why. And maybe there was a connection. That tape! The closest thing to actual evidence they'd found so far. Although there'd been nothing on the tape to identify the intruder, they knew now that there had indeed been one. Whatever had happened to Mrs. Littlefield had apparently begun somehow out there in the barn. And now the Rafferty girls. They, too, had been in the barn.

If only Mrs. Littlefield hadn't been so quick to turn off her damn machine! Ah, well. He thought about that some more. If Hillary Littlefield, as smart and feisty as she was, had felt any kind of threat to her safety, wouldn't she have had the presence of mind to leave the cassette recorder on?

He wanted to listen to the tape again. Her tone of voice seemed to indicate a kind of contempt for the person who had entered. Contempt and recognition. It was someone she knew and felt superior to. Somebody Mrs. Littlefield knew. Somebody they all knew?

Had the same thing happened to the little Rafferty girls? Had somebody entered the barn . . . lured them out on some pretext? But they were still alive. They had to be. They were either out there in the woods somewhere . . . or being held against their will.

The constable entered the main house through the back door. Jake Charpentier was seated at the kitchen table examining a copy of the 1956 Indian Meadow survey map that included all of the Perry house property. Madeleine and Rose and several other women had begun to serve coffee and sandwiches. People were starting to mill about, grabbing a hurried cup of coffee, exchanging information, regrouping.

Jake was intently tracing the path of the stream down from the pond with his finger. The map called it Quaker Creek because it connected Little Quaker Pond to Big Quaker Pond some four miles or so to the north. But he'd never heard anybody use that name for it. It was, simply, "the pond stream" or "the creek."

Jake looked up when Emmett Wilbur came in. "Take a look at this, Constable," he invited. Wilbur came to where Jake sat and looked over his shoulder. "I've been thinking, sir, with everybody covering all the trails, it might be a good idea for somebody—me—to cover the creek bed. Follow it from that beaver dam all the way back to where it eventually hits the town road at that culvert over by Thompson's camp. It's two or three miles, near as I can make out."

A group of volunteers had just come in, and Rose and Madeleine were attending to them. Jake lowered his voice. "I mean, I don't expect we'll find 'em *in* the water—God forbid!—but this is the only way I can see to cover a great big patch of land that's got no trails goin' through it. See, I don't figure those kids know the trails. And since we don't know what got 'em lost to begin with, we can't rule out an area just because it's got no trails leading through it. This here's some four or five square miles we're talkin' about. Eh? What do you think?"

Wilbur's brief spate of hopefulness evaporated. He could suddenly picture how very small those two little girls were. So small that if they had fallen into the creek, the way Hillary Littlefield had apparently done, they might not have been carried all the way to the dam. Any small obstacle could stop them. A submerged log. A large boulder. Anything.

His heart once again filled with rank foreboding, Wilbur told Jake yes. The creek had to be searched. And who better qualified to do it than this strapping fellow who'd learned his amazing survival skills while engaged in a host of questionable youthful escapades?

Jake thanked him. He knew it would be sheer hell to accomplish what he had just proposed. He'd be slogging two or three slippery, wet, rocky, twisty, uphill miles without the prospect of a single viable foothold. Real rough, unfriendly ground . . . in damn poor visibility. Fog and mist, mostly; the rain looked like it was finally slackening off. He wondered if it could be done. He knew nobody else here could do it. It was going to be up to him: good ol' Jake Charpentier, master tracker, ace mountaineer, and all-around woodsman. Because for sure nobody could possibly feel worse about those two missing little girls than he did.

He got up from the table, gave Rose a quick kiss on the cheek, and left the dry, warm kitchen. Then he went out to the van to get his gear together.

Rose kept darting furtive little glances over at Madeleine to see how she was doing. Was this the right way for her to deal with what she must be feeling? Making coffee, piling sandwiches up on platters? Who was to say? Keeping busy, being surrounded by all these good people certainly helped her, so maybe it was good for Madeleine, too. She needed to say something to her but was afraid she'd get it wrong. Still, she had to try.

"Uh, Madeleine . . . when this is all behind us, and we have them home safe with us again . . . I'll try to tell you how it . . . I mean, explain why . . ."

"Rose. Not needed. Honest. Nobody can watch kids every minute of the day. Whatever's h-happened to them . . . it could have happened while I was here, too. It isn't your f-fault. I don't know whose fault it is, but I know it's not yours—or Jake's. Please, let's not talk about it anymore. I can't . . ."

Rose gave Madeleine's shoulder a light squeeze, and then she turned away and busied herself with the coffeemaker. She couldn't let herself dwell on Tillie and Libby, could not permit herself to picture their sweet, familiar little faces, because whenever she did, she saw them with such piercing clarity—looking so scared, so abandoned! If they'd managed to work their way into her heart this deep in just three short weeks—how must it be for Madeleine?

Madeleine was saying, "Yes, these all have mustard, and those mayonnaise. There's some ketchup and Russian dressing over here . . . and pickles—"

And then all of a sudden Madeleine thought of something. God knew where the thought had come from, because she wasn't aware she'd been thinking at all. In fact she had very carefully *not* been thinking. She had no conscious memory of the orange BMW in the parking lot of the Blue Mirror Café. But it suddenly occurred to her that Libby and Tillie could have been *abducted*! By their father.

She looked around the room, spotting Constable Wilbur over by the table going over some notes. Jake had apparently gone out again.

"Constable Wilbur, could I speak to you for a moment? I've just thought of something."

She blurted it out as soon as the door to the front room was safely closed behind them. "This could be their father's doing. I don't know why I didn't think of it before. He contacted some friends of mine. He made threatening remarks." She explained about Matt and Sylvie's phone call.

"Well, we can check that out quick enough. Do you have a number where he can be reached?"

"I can't call him. I just can't."

"I'll do it. Let's have that number."

They went back to the phone in the kitchen and Wilbur dialed the New York City number. He heard it ring once, and then heard the answering machine click on.

"Hello, this is Gilbert Rafferty speaking," it said. "I am out of town on assignment at present and shall be away from the studio for some time. . . ." Emmett held the receiver up to Madeleine, and she heard Gil wind up his message with, "At the tone, please leave your name and number, and I will get back to you." They heard it through a second time. They did not leave a message. Madeleine, who had at first shrunk back from having to hear Gil speak, then hardened herself in order to hear the message through again. She had recognized, as only she could, the unmistakable, smarmy, phony voice Gil used when he lied. She shuddered.

"He's lying. He's not on an assignment. He could have come up here."

Constable Wilbur believed her, but it didn't change anything. They still didn't know who or what they were looking for. They would have to keep on searching, that's all. He patted Madeleine's back a bit awkwardly and excused himself, stepping out into the white misty quiet to summon the troopers from the police radio in his car.

As Libby continued to tell her story about some children who lived in the woods and gathered nuts and berries to eat and never had to go to school, Tillie tried to get more com-

150

fortable, looking in vain for some position that would make her foot hurt less. She tried resting her head in her sister's lap, and that seemed to feel a little better. By the time Tillie finally fell asleep, Libby's voice had deteriorated to a hoarse whisper, and her throat really hurt.

Having Tillie asleep made Libby feel lonely. Every now and then she thought she heard voices far away. But she couldn't be sure. Mommy and Rose had to be out looking for them. But it had been such a long time. It had to be at least dinnertime by now.

While she couldn't be sure about the voices, she was definitely sure she heard cars swishing by on a wet road. She couldn't see them or anything, but whenever cars and trucks would come along—which wasn't all that often—they sounded just about as close as they did from up at the house. Tillie was shivering in her sleep. Libby didn't know what to do.

She kept remembering their safety-rule poster on the refrigerator door. Number One: Never go into the woods alone. Tillie's foot was really hurt, and there was no way she could carry her. If she left Tillie here alone to try to make it to that road and get help, how would Tillie manage? She even considered just leaving her there, asleep, and trying for the road. She might get back again with somebody to help them even before Tillie woke up. But she discounted that immediately. Imagine waking up in the woods all by yourself with a foot that hurt too much to walk on!

How could she get help to come back here? She had no idea where they were! There was nothing to distinguish this patch of woods from any other. There was a pretty big stream back there, somewhere. She could hear it roaring by. But she couldn't see it. She looked around at the little grove of pine trees, the lichen-covered grayish rocks, the mist-enshrouded treetops. Maybe on a sunny day she could have seen something to mark their whereabouts, but today there was nothing.

And then she figured out what she could do. When she got to the road, she could tie her shirt to a tree at the edge of it. With grown-ups along to help, that would be enough to find their way back to Tillie. But figuring out how to do it and actually doing it were two different things. She'd let Tillie sleep awhile. They were safe here. It was like they were sitting in the middle of this big fluffy cloud. And then Libby dozed off.

By five o'clock, Gilbert Rafferty began to see signs that said Elizabethtown and Keene and Lake Placid. He pulled over to the side of the road and reread the directions he'd got from that lady at the realty office. Had they been wrong? Had the poor visibility caused him to miss a turn? He had to admit he'd let his mind wander during the last few miles.

He'd been trying to come up with some plan for dealing with Madeleine. Now that he was getting closer and closer to the event, he realized that he really didn't want to see her. He could picture all too plainly the belligerent, ugly expression that would come on her face the second she opened the door to him. She was not about to welcome him with open arms. He was all too well aware of that! His left hand unconsciously touched the scar on his forehead. Madeleine was a dead issue. Nothing left there . . . no glowing embers to fan back to life.

But she had his children hidden away up here in some godforsaken out-of-the-way cabin! Elizabeth and Matilda. They were as much his as they were hers, damn it! Still, he didn't think it would be a good idea to call first. Surprise would definitely work to his advantage. That was about as far as he had come in his planning when he realized he must have bypassed the place entirely. He turned back.

This time, he'd keep his eyes glued to the road. What he was looking for was a dirt drive that forked to the left after a low stone wall, about four miles up from the village. Had he taken the wrong road out of town? He decided to drive all the way back to Indian Meadow and start over. He was beginning to think maybe he'd taken a left at the Mobil station where he should have hung a right. It was a mistake anyone could have made. Besides, that weird woman's handwriting was hard to make out.

CHAPTER

17

GIL had turned on his foglights, but they weren't doing much good. Could be one of them was burned out; he hadn't checked lately. The fog had a way of swooping up on him unexpectedly. One minute the road would be clear, and then the next, he'd round a curve and find himself absolutely blinded. As it was, he was only doing about twenty-five miles an hour. He tried turning the headlights on. That seemed to help.

This had to be the right road. It had been winding steadily uphill, and there was a hidden-away, deserted feel to it. No derelict tourist cabins or down-at-the-heel antique stands like that other road he'd been on. He even caught glimpses of animals from time to time. Little forest creatures! His headlights would catch their eyes . . . transfixing them with an eerie phosphorescence. He'd seen raccoons, a red fox, and some funny, scrawny little things that looked like prairie dogs—coyotes? Did they have those up here?

He wondered if he'd see anything really big, like a deer

or a moose . . . or a bear! *Lions and tigers and bears, oh my!* This was kind of fun.

Cautiously, he rounded the next curve. There was a scurrying movement over to the left. Some animal or other. No, by God! He couldn't believe his eyes. It looked just like a little naked child! Had he dozed off behind the wheel? God knew, he'd been up since dawn, driving practically all day. No, that's what it was. There was a naked child standing alone in the swirling fog up ahead. The child was waving its skinny brown arms at him.

When Libby saw the car, she saw a pair of headlights mostly and a grille. It wasn't until it began to slow down and pull over that she even realized it was orange. It never once occurred to her that it might be Daddy's car. When the man stopped and got out she still didn't recognize him. For some dumb reason she'd been looking at the pair of feet stepping down behind the opened door.

Gil saw the red-framed eyeglasses on the little lost child's nose. "Oh my God! Elizabeth!"

Libby realized who it was, and everything seemed to stop. She closed her eyes. She didn't want to see him, couldn't bear to look at him.

"My *God,* look at you! What's happened to your clothes? Is this how your mother takes care of you up here? You look like a wild thing!" Gil was as upset as Libby was. He didn't know what he was saying. He couldn't quite believe this was happening. He went to put his arm around her protectively and she flinched.

"Let me go!" she shouted. Of all the grown-ups to come driving up . . . why *him?* He was even worse than that awful Missie! Why was this happening? Weren't there any good people left in the world? Where was Mommy? Where was Rose?

"Where is Matilda? What have you done to her?"

"Don't touch me! Get away from me!"

Now it was starting to sink in. His daughter wasn't reacting nearly as much to him, personally, as she was to having been lost, to being alone here by the side of the road. She obviously didn't know what she was saying or doing. He had to comfort her, soften her up a little, snap her out of it.

"Libby! Sweetheart, it's Daddy. Don't you even recognize me? Whatever has happened? Why are your pants all torn like that, and what happened to your shirt?"

"Aw, it was all wet. I just took it off, I guess."

"Thank God I've come along. I can help. First things first. Let me get you a sweater. Then I'll take you home. Okay? Everything's going to be all right. Daddy's here."

He reached into the backseat for the old moth-eaten sweater he always kept there for just such an emergency. First he used it to pat Libby dry. She endured these ministrations, but she shrank from his smell, the Daddy smell that she'd endured so often before, his particular combination of thick, sweetish after-shave, stale sweat, and day-old whiskey. The smell reminded her of things she'd almost managed to forget.

When he tried to pull the sweater over her head, she turned away. "Give me it. I'll do it," she muttered hoarsely. Libby simply couldn't stand another minute of his touching her. She grabbed the sweater roughly out of his hands and tied the long sleeves carelessly around her neck. Satisfied that his generosity had been accepted, Gil opened the passenger door with a mock formal, "Where to, miss?"

"I don't know," she said. "I was in the woods. I just got to the road when . . . when you came."

"Hop in. I've got some directions. We'll find it."

Libby hesitated. She remembered what she'd overheard Mommy saying to Rose the other night on the porch. About him coming and maybe taking them away.

"Elizabeth? Are you coming, child?"

Libby decided she didn't want him going into the woods with her to rescue Tillie. He wasn't safe. They might find themselves stuck in the car with him, going back to the city.

156

These were images, not thoughts. Let Mommy and Rose come for Tillie. That would be better.

"If I get in, you have to promise you'll take me straight to the Perry house!"

"The Perry house? Oh, you mean the cabin you're staying at! Well, of course, where else would I take you? Your mother must be worried sick about you!"

Wasn't it absolutely providential the way things sometimes worked out? he thought. Here he'd been worried about how best to approach Madeleine, and now he would be given a regular hero's welcome!

But why was Libby still looking at him with such crazy scared eyes? "Hey, little lady, why so solemn? One would think I was planning to *abscond* with you!" He laughed at his choice of word—a word Libby did not understand. But she understood the laugh. It was a distancing, arrogant laugh . . . the sort of laugh children often get from grown-ups who are uncomfortable around them. She had a flash of memory . . . the last time she'd heard him laugh in just that way.

Glancing over her shoulder in the direction of the injured sister she was leaving behind, Libby entered her father's car. She closed her eyes and silently swore to keep her promise. She would get help to Tillie! Just as soon as she found her way back to Mommy.

In the car, Libby's mind drifted. It had been more than three hours since Missie first joined them in the toy barn, and she was exhausted. There wasn't enough of her left to absorb this latest circumstance. She sat there and actually forgot, for a moment, that it was her father sitting over there in the driver's seat. The whole time she'd been slogging through the wet woods, trying to find the road, trying to get help for Tillie, she'd had this idea of what it would be like when she was rescued. Some nice person would stop his car for her, would drive her to safety. Sitting there warm and dry while the car crept carefully along the foggy road, she forgot that it hadn't exactly turned out that way. That it wasn't some nice imaginary person driving this car. That it was her father, whom she hated.

Gil's concentration on the road kept him from even looking her way. Then, after quite some time had passed, he said, "Actually, Elizabeth, I think we must nearly be there. . . ."

Libby looked out through the fog. She felt a flood of relief. They were! They were almost home! They were just turning the bend in the road before you saw the driveway. There was the toy barn! Its peaked slate roof, the window in the gable all lit up!

"There!" she croaked. She might have said, "There's the toy barn!" Or, "We're nearly there!" But "There!" was all her scratchy voice seemed to manage.

And Gil, having interpreted that to mean "There's the house," pulled over, drove up a little way along the rough, overgrown wagon road, and came to a jolting stop behind one of the many sheds abounding on the Perry house property. He mistook the brightly lit barn up ahead for the house itself. He couldn't believe Madeleine would let her children live in such backwoods squalor. And yet he was glad to believe it. A sign of her total inability to be left in charge of their care! He could already visualize how indefensible this situation could be made to seem, typed up just so on a legal document. An unfit mother!

Libby didn't know why they were stopping here. Had her father seen somebody? Was Rose out here looking for Tillie and her? She got out and walked up toward the barn. They were approaching it across a small clearing, down from the actual path.

Light—magically transformed by the fog—beckoned through the partially opened doors. There was a heightened reality to the moment—seeing that building looking so solid and familiar after all those hours when nothing had been either familiar or solid—and yet at the same time, the barn gave Libby an unsteady dizzying sensa-

158

tion, a feeling that it might at any moment float just out of her reach, sail off into the gauzy sea of mist that surrounded it. She tripped. Gil caught her. He kept his hand under her arm to steady her.

They walked in.

Libby stepped ahead of her father, looking around to see if anyone was there. "Rose? Mommy?" The barn showed signs of many people having recently been there. Been there and gone. There were things left lying around in places that were usually empty. A table had been set up in the middle of the large empty space by the door. There were paper napkins with half-eaten sandwiches on them, a couple of empty paper cups, opened maps and papers lying about on the floor.

"Elizabeth? What is this? You live here? You live in this place? Where do you sleep? Where's the kitchen? Where are your mother and sister?" Gil, walking in behind her, simply could not take in what he was looking at.

Libby shook her head no. "It's the toy barn. We play here." Her throat hurt real bad. Her voice was a hoarse squeak.

Now he saw. He saw all the shelves, all the artifacts hanging from the rafters. Why, this place was amazing! It was fantastic! What a find! Antique toys! Props! Yards and yards of fabulous props!

"Oh, Libby! This is terrific! Think of the pictures I could take here! You and Tillie, dressed in cute little period costumes, posing for me with all these toys! My two very best models, eh? What a *gold mine*! How did your mother ever find this place?" He wanted to stay. Move in. Reconcile with Madeleine. A whole new amazing series of pictures! Nostalgia was big. A coffee table book for the Christmas market . . . he could *see* it! His mind was alive with the charming, colorful possibilities. Talk about serendipity!

Libby tried not to listen. She found herself drawn, inexorably, to the spot behind the steps to the hayloft. The two cartons were back in place.

Gil came up behind her.

"And what's back here?" He asked.

"Down there." She pointed, her cracked voice barely audible. She tried to step out of his way, but he was coming up right behind her, crowding her.

"What do you mean, down?"

"Tillie and me were down there," she whispered. "Under those."

"You mean under those boxes?" Gil pushed roughly past Libby.

Once again she smelled his strong scent. She remembered the way he smelled when he worked under those hot lights at the studio, when he posed her and Tillie for pictures, touching her in that clammy, flat-palmed way he had that made her skin crawl. He'd fuss over the costume for what seemed like hours, telling her to hold still, not to fidget, until sometimes, by the time all the adjustments had been made to his complete satisfaction, she was in tears. And of course that would drive him into a rage! He'd shout at her, order her to go and wash her face, and then they'd have to start all over again. She didn't ever want to have to go through that again! Not any of it!

She remembered the strange man looking at her. She remembered the things he said.

She hadn't seen him at first, and then suddenly there he was, dressed in some kind of robe that he'd left hanging open. Daddy had taken off her glasses for the photo session, so she couldn't see all that well. But she could see well enough to know that he had nothing on underneath. And well enough to realize that the big hairy mess he had down there didn't look like anything she'd ever seen. He was standing next to Daddy and they were looking at her through the camera, laughing. Daddy's eyes had that dark, shiny, dancing look they sometimes got. And he kept sniffing all the time, like he had a runny nose or something.

Daddy had told her simply to let go and dance up a storm

to the music playing on the stereo. He slipped off the gauzy black tutu she'd been wearing, leaving just the stretchy black stockings rolled down her little thighs. "Bend down!" he'd say. "Look back up at me through your legs!" And, feeling her hair brush the floor, her cheeks flush as the blood rushed to them, listening with pride to the repeated approbation of the clicking shutter, she would. The lights felt so warm, and they were all pink, and she felt very special—like a famous TV star—dancing all alone in front of that huge sparkly white backdrop.

Then she saw the man in the robe, standing next to Daddy, looking through the big camera on its tripod. The man was saying, so she could hear, "Mmm mmm, will you look at that! Can there be a sweeter sight in all the world than an unspoiled little pink cunt? All neat and plump and hairless?"

"Shame on you, Lance. You're an incorrigible pedophile!" Daddy had answered, laughing that laugh.

At first she'd glowed with pleasure and continued dancing, rather self-consciously, to win even more approval. She didn't understand the words, only that she was being praised. But then, something inside her must have understood. She felt something odd, something dangerous, as sharp as a pain. And then, without realizing what she was doing, she stopped dancing. In that startled instant, she stood there, her shoulders hunching forward as though she'd been struck in the back, her face looking up at Daddy in wide-eyed betrayal, her hands meeting reflexively to cover the private place just inches above the tops of the rolled black stockings.

The flash blazed. The camera clicked.

"A good one!" Daddy said with satisfaction.

Daddy was pushing and kicking the boxes roughly aside before Libby could say more. He found the trapdoor, discovered the knothole, poked his fingers through, and raised up the door. When he saw the steps, the gloom, the dank,

161

he began to mutter incredulously, "I can't believe this! D'you mean to tell me you and Tillie were actually permitted to *play* down there? That's outrageous! I can't believe this! Your mother must be losing her bloody mind!" He was standing there on the first stone step, holding the wooden lid open with one hand, unaware of the hook to which it could be fastened on the wooden stairs above him.

She hated it when he said bad things about Mom. "No!" she squeaked indignantly. She tried again. A stage whisper this time. "No, Daddy! It wasn't like that. This bad lady, she shoved Tillie and me in there. It was awful. When you came, I was going for help. Tillie's *hurt.*" The extraordinary effort of speaking had caused her to say more than she'd meant to. She hadn't wanted him to know about Tillie. By now she'd begun to cry really hard.

Gil barely understood a word she'd said. But in his typically fragmented way, he'd reacted to a simple red warning light that had gone off in his head. Tillie was *hurt* . . . and she was down those steps! Thank God he'd come along when he did! "Tillie? Tillie! Oh my God, *Matilda*! Hold on, your daddy's coming."

Why was he going down the steps? "No, Daddy! Not down there! Tillie isn't down there!" But no sound came out of her mouth. No sound at all. Her throat had closed completely.

Daddy was already half out of sight when she ran across the short distance between them to try to stop him.

Gil lunged impulsively down the dark uneven steps, pushing back the hatch behind him so it would fall back open. Considering his haste, the lack of a handrail, and the guarded condition of his thin-soled Italian shoes, it was perhaps inevitable that he should lose his footing. It was Gil's fatal misfortune, however, that he did so immediately—while his fingers were still stuck in the hatch.

And so it fell forward—not back.

Libby drew alongside just as it slammed shut with a loud bang. "No, Daddy!" she mouthed helplessly. "Daddy, no!

Come back!" Though there had been one terrible high-pitched shriek of pain, she could not know that her father had landed full force at the bottom of the rough stone steps, with his legs twisted grotesquely beneath him.

Sobbing uncontrollably, Libby poked her hands into the hole and tried to lift up the thick wooden trapdoor. Little choking glottal noises were coming out of her, comprised in equal part of effort and tears. Her hands were not strong enough. She wasn't strong enough. Her small body had completely exhausted itself. As Libby continued her ineffectual struggle with the unyielding slab of wood, the choking gasping noises of her own waterlogged sobs gradually became louder in her ears than that single remembered scream.

Eventually, she had to stop trying.

She'd been sprawled on the floor by the closed trapdoor, and now her head simply fell down on her outstretched arm. Her eyes fluttered and closed.

And then all the pictures that had been crowding her mind so painfully, all the starkly remembered images of the terrible things that had happened to her in that single afternoon began to recede. And that felt better. The smaller the pictures got, the less they hurt. So she let them get smaller and smaller and smaller and smaller until, like the blue-white pinpoint of a turned-off TV, they disappeared altogether. . . .

And mercifully, the dry spasmodic sobs that continued to shake her little body were at last replaced by the soft rise and fall of deep dreamless sleep.

Some minutes later, when Libby's eyes opened, her head no longer hurt. She sat up, almost unaware that she'd been asleep, and rose quickly to do what she knew she had to do.

She had to get help for Tillie.

CHAPTER

18

JAKE Charpentier had been gone for nearly an hour.

Two state troopers were on their way out to Indian Meadow: one from Elizabethtown and one driving up from where he'd been cruising the Northway near exit 28. If the children weren't found soon after that, they would alert EnCon and call the rangers in, while there was still an hour or two of daylight left. All of the assembled friends, neighbors, and volunteer firemen had had their coffee and sandwiches, exchanged whatever intelligence there was, and gone back to the search. Constable Wilbur's command post was in his car, by his police radio. A copy of the survey map lay partially unfolded in front of him, pushed up against the steering wheel. He'd marked the various areas off in grease pencil and written in the names of the people covering them.

If those girls were in the woods, and alive, they would be found soon. If they had met with the same misfortune as Hillary Littlefield, their bodies might not be discovered for days. He winced as a picture came to him of Jake finding first one and then another ghastly small body—twisted into some awful distorted position—lodged in the water, under a rock, or in the crook of a dead branch. Ahh, no! Please! Children got lost all the time. And found all the time, too. More often than not, hardly the worse for wear.

Madeleine had stayed in the kitchen, helping Rose and the other women—Jeannine Devereaux from the IGA Grocery, Mabel Thompson, their closest neighbor down the road, whom she had not met before—clean up. They held off putting on more coffee or making more sandwiches. Their attitude, at least around Madeleine, was that the girls would most certainly be found before this would become necessary.

"You know, dear," Mabel was saying to Madeleine now, as though they'd known each other for years, "if it weren't for this nasty fog, your girls would probably already be sitting here, safe and sound. I remember that summer when my two decided to take a hike. Nine and twelve they were at the time. Why, we had half of Indian Meadow out there, looking for 'em. They were finally found less than half a mile from home—though of course the poor kids never knew it. It was pretty foggy that day, too. A lot like today. There's nothing worse than the waiting. But once it's over, once they're found . . . well, you'll be so happy, you'll forget how awful this part was." Mabel leaned over and threw a substantial arm around Madeleine. Though her words, happy ending and all, might have sounded a bit patronizing, her face expressed sincere compassion and concern.

Found! How would they be when they were found? Madeleine couldn't let herself think of, couldn't let herself imagine all the possibilities that loomed out there unknown to her in the forest. Whatever might have befallen them had already happened. Whatever condition they were in now, that was how they would be when they were found.

"I'm going out for some air." She walked out on the

porch and down the steps. Once again the front yard was full of cars, vans, and pickup trucks. But for the wisps of fog that today obscured their outlines, the scene was reminiscent of that other time, when Hillary Littlefield had been found. She wouldn't let herself think about that. How was she going to get through this? If she could, she'd have joined the searchers, marching right off into the woods, herself. But they'd only end up having to search for her, as well.

She began to walk down the path to the pond. She passed the empty toy barn on her left, still all lit up, and considered going in. She decided against it. It felt better to be out of doors, somehow. If Libby and Tillie were out there somewhere, well, at least she could try to feel what they must be feeling. It had stopped raining, but the fog was a heavy wet moving cloud that coated her with damp from head to foot in seconds. If they *were* out there, they'd soon be suffering from exposure. Oh, please God, let that be all they were suffering from!

Madeleine continued walking until she got to the pond. She knelt down by the edge of the calm water. It was so quiet here. A water bug, its transparent weblike wings festooned with droplets like a tiny string of lights, made its way across the surface, leaving a feathery little wake behind it. The sight of it—its delicacy, its calm purposefulness—filled her with hope. Or maybe it was just the grateful knowledge that Libby and Tillie had not been found here! Didn't that mean that this wasn't "Hillary Littlefield all over again" as people had said at first? She'd heard them. They were only giving voice to what she'd been thinking herself. But this time the pond had been innocent. And that's how it looked to her now: all silvery white in the heavy fog . . . innocent . . . benign. Madeleine walked up to the splintery old wooden dock and sat down. She would wait here.

For as long as it took.

166

*　　*　　*

If his purpose had not been so serious and urgent, Jake Charpentier might actually have been enjoying himself. The terrain was not without hazards, but so far there was nothing he wasn't equipped to handle with dispatch. He'd been making excellent time. He'd decided against wearing waders, and he didn't own a wet suit. He was dressed in climbing shorts, wearing an old reliable pair of duck boots that fit well and provided some traction underfoot as well as support for his ankles. He had nylon line and climbing gear in his pack; so far, he hadn't needed it. He'd been following the creek, and it had been a steady, gradual trek uphill—wading right through the water, testing each and every footfall before taking it.

Trying to bushwhack through the shoreline on either side would have taken twice as long. He kept calling out Libby and Tillie's names, shouting "Halloo!" and listening for any response. He'd fallen down a few times and lost his ground completely once, spinning swiftly back some hundred yards or so, like a hapless piece of floating debris, before catching hold of an overhanging branch. But he'd never felt in serious danger. He was good at this. And he was seeing a part of these woods he had never seen before.

The first thing he discovered was that the survey map was no use to him at all. It indicated the creek traveling a fairly straight path, north to south. Not so. It meandered gently, now one way, now another. And its true direction was from the northwest toward the southeast. The land to either side of it had been carved out by the force of the water, sheer slopes as high as twenty or thirty feet. And then, once in a while, he'd pass a section where the water had deposited the beginnings of a curved gravelly beach. There was much evidence of heavy—and ongoing—flooding.

So far there had been no sudden cliffs to scale, no roaring waterfall to stop his progress. It was like going up a series of more or less manageable steps. But he kept his

167

ears pricked up, just in case such a fall might still lie up ahead. He also kept listening for an answer to his regular calling out. And sometimes some animal or bird would fool him: make him think for a minute that he'd found 'em. His heart would start to beat like a trip-hammer! Those were the moments he had to be the most careful of; one second's lapse could really cost him here.

Then he reached the slide. A massive mudslide. Brandnew. To the left of him, about twenty feet from shore. In fact, it looked so new, he feared it might still be in progress. The creek was busy encroaching it, bubbling up, churning slickly like something viscous, sloughing over to the left to claim what had until recently been dry land.

Huge boulders and rocks were all tumbled in over one another, trees were pulled down, enormous roots up in the air, the mud clinging to their tendrils torn so recently from the ground it had not weathered. Jake was scared now. Whatever had caused the slide, and he couldn't tell standing there in the middle of the water, what that might have been, could still be going on.

He was scared for himself, and he was scared for the girls. Could this be what had happened to them? He had to get over there. He decided to veer over to shore on the right, move forward—very cautiously—beyond the immediate area of the slide, and then cross over and double back. As he made his way slowly past it, he saw that it looked like an enormous sink hole. Like the ground had just opened up and the water claimed it—was still claiming it. Perhaps this had been a juncture with an underground stream. All the heavy rain could have dissolved whatever had been keeping the two bodies of water apart. As he pulled ahead of the slide and prepared to cross over to shore safely upstream of it, he heard a low, grinding noise. Somewhere down below, the ground was still moving. He felt it tremble through his feet. Very carefully then, he made his way up the muddy bank.

Beyond the scraggly, tangled briars on the edge of the

now extremely turbulent creek, he came into some pinewoods. It was an actual grove, affording him a much safer access than he'd hoped for. He started across the soft damp bed of pine needles, and then he stopped. He'd heard somthing. A raspy, high-pitched little voice. This time he knew it was not an animal or a bird. Tunelessly, listlessly, it was singing.

"This old man, he played three, he played knick-knack on his knee!"

Harry Littlefield had finished covering the area he'd been assigned, a steep slope that ended near the trailhead to Stoddard Mountain. He'd found nothing. He'd parked his Cherokee down the road and now walked back to it, feeling anxious and discouraged. He could hear voices of other searchers nearby. It must be nearly six o'clock. The girls had been missing for some three and a half hours.

He checked in with Constable Wilbur, leaning on his car, talking through the opened window. The troopers had arrived and gone into the woods, armed with walkie-talkies. You could hear them squawking through the constable's radio. Nothing so far.

Then Rose came rushing out the kitchen door, running toward them. Neither Littlefield nor Wilbur could tell from her face whether the news was good or bad. It all came tumbling out of her in breathless half-finished sentences. Charpentier had telephoned from the Thompsons' camp. He'd found Tillie! She had an injured foot—probably broken—and she was running a fever. But she'd be all right.

"And Libby, what about her? What did Jake have to say about her?"

"He said she was probably okay. Tillie said she'd gone for help. . . . Isn't Madeleine out here with you? I thought she was. She doesn't know yet!"

"I saw her walk by awhile ago, going that way, down toward the pond," Wilbur said. "You want me to go tell her?"

Littlefield said, "Let me."

Rose stood there and watched him go. Wilbur saw the look on her face.

"You know, Rose," he said, "I think there's going to be a happy ending to this one."

Harry Littlefield hurried toward the pond, almost jogging along the narrow, bumpy path. Where was she? Was she all right? While he could easily understand why she'd chosen to wait it out alone, he found himself—admittedly, somewhat irrationally—suddenly fearful for *her* safety. Should they have let her stray from sight for so long? Then he saw the pond peek through the trees in the fog, and then the quiet, silhouetted figure sitting on the dock. The lady was fine. Her children would be, too. He just knew they would.

She didn't see him until he was within a few feet of the dock. Oh God. News. Good or bad? She couldn't see his face. She stood up, her hands in front of her mouth, her eyes wide and dark with dread.

"Madeleine!"

He walked up to her on the dock and took her hands gently away from her face, holding them in his own. "Madeleine. Jake phoned from the Thompsons'. He has Tillie. Libby left her to get help. It should be just a matter of time before she's found, too."

Her eyes waited for more.

"She's fine, Madeleine. She hurt her foot. That's why Libby left her to go get help, but she's fine."

Madeleine's knees sank. She felt as though all her bones had come undone. Harry caught her awkwardly, barely keeping her from falling.

"It's all right, really! I'm not going to faint . . . I don't think . . ." But the world was spinning—a misty whirlwind, blinding white. The relief was so strong, so enormous, it felt like a thunderclap had gone off inside her.

Harry kept his arms around her, supporting her lest she topple backward. There seemed to be no weight to her at

170

all, but at the same time there was this lovely sense of roundness, of yielding softness, in the way she felt to hold. Instead of letting go as she began to recover from the initial shock, he adjusted his hold on her, circling his arms around her more securely. Her face was so close. . . .

Madeleine found herself unable to turn her gaze away from the eyes that had suddenly come so close. There was a kind of terror to such closeness. And only one way to stop it. She kissed Harry.

There was no strangeness, no terror, to the kiss. No clicking of teeth, no scratching of an unfamiliar masculine cheek, nothing but two mouths meeting—weightless, timeless, intent. Again and again.

Madeleine pulled away.

"No! I can't let myself go . . . not yet . . . not when Libby's still out there!" But they kissed again. She pulled away once more. "How can I do this . . . how can I let myself feel this . . . this, oh, Harry, this wonderful . . . when I still don't know that she's safe?"

"It is wonderful. We're going to be all right. I know it. You can let go now, Madeleine. Just let go." And this time when Harry kissed her, she did not pull away. The tart clean geranium-petal taste of the inside of his mouth—so new to her and yet already so known—had become absolutely necessary. Madeleine had let go.

Emmett Wilbur was sitting in his car talking to the troopers on their walkie-talkie channel, telling them the good news about Tillie.

"We haven't found the older girl yet, but her sister said she was heading for the road, so it should be just a matter of time—" Then he said, "Uh, wait a minute, I just spotted something. . . ."

A little half-naked child was walking up the drive.

"She's here! She's walking up the drive right now! The search is over, guys! Call everybody in." He was so excited he began to honk his horn repeatedly. That sent Rose running out the front door again at full speed. She got to Libby before anybody else could.

Pretty soon, searchers began coming out of the woods, convening in the Perry house front yard. One by one, and in pairs, they would make their way to their cars to add their own individual notes to the overall horn-honking jubilation.

CHAPTER
19

JOE Mitford was driving back from the remote, run-down hunting camp he had shown to the couple from Hartford. The place needed lots of work—but they'd been told that up front. No electricity, no real road. Forty prime acres of forest land that included a small marshy pond that could easily be dug out and made into a beautiful private swimming hole. And the price was an absolute steal. He'd told them all this over the phone; he hadn't tried to gild the lily at all.

They'd hated it. The weather sure hadn't helped—unrelenting rain. When they finally arrived—after he'd twice missed the turnoff—the woman had sunk in mud up to her ankles merely on stepping out of the car. And it only got worse after that. She'd kept staring at his face as though he disgusted her. As though his exotropic eyes were a personal insult to her. Oh, well. He certainly had experienced that before. Maybe Mother's appointment had been more productive. This had been the second visit for those gentlemen from New York. They were looking at a great big turn-of-the-century camp for possible conversion into a corporate conference center. What a commission that would be!

He'd been away from the office for hours. He was worried that Missie might never have showed up. She hadn't been there at three like she'd promised. He'd had to lock up, leave the place dark. He decided to drive by now, check things out, even though it was after six.

As he got closer to town, he heard car horns tooting and honking repeatedly off in the distance. A wedding. An experience that would no doubt forever be denied to him. He heaved a heavy, lugubrious sigh. Why, even his crazy sister Missie had at least managed that much; never mind it didn't work out. Strange, he thought, nobody getting married 'round these parts that he knew of. Must be weekend or summer folks.

Libby sat in the brightly lit kitchen wrapped in a robe, a light cotton blanket across her lap. She felt calm, sick, safe, and strange. She was burning up with fever. Rose was pouring some orange juice into a glass for her.

"Here, drink this, sweetie." Rose handed her the glass and gave her yet another hug. She wrapped the robe around her more securely, tucked the blanket under her legs. "I can't understand why you didn't even have a shirt on. You've caught yourself a real bad cold."

"Aw, it was all torn and hanging down and wet anyway. I just took it off, I guess," Libby whispered. She drank the juice. It stung her throat going down.

By the time her mother and Harry Littlefield ran breathlessly into the room, Rose had taken her temperature and given her aspirin to go with the orange juice.

Although it hurt her throat to talk, she tried to repeat her story again for them. Mommy was so glad to see her, she just kept hugging and kissing her and saying things like "It's all right! You're both all right now. That's all that matters!" She was crying and laughing at the same time.

Finally, Libby asked hoarsely, "How soon before Tillie

174

gets here?" She really wanted to see Tillie. Of everything that had happened, it now seemed to her that having to leave Tillie behind all alone like that had been the scariest thing of all.

"Jake's taken her to the emergency room up in Lake Placid. He thinks her foot may be broken, honey."

"How soon before she gets back?"

"We don't know, sweetie. We're on our way up there right now."

"Can't I come too?"

"Libby, you've got a fever of a hundred and three degrees and a terrible case of laryngitis, so you'd better stay here, all cozy and safe, and get better, okay?" Madeleine searched Libby's flushed face. Her expression seemed altered, something about her eyes. How had she managed to endure all that she'd gone through . . . all alone, nobody to help her?

"Okay." Actually Libby was feeling pretty tired. She walked over to the big overstuffed sofa in the living room and settled into the pillows. Madeleine followed her, covering her with the blanket she'd let slide down behind her on the kitchen floor. She sat down next to her to kiss her good-bye. Madeleine hadn't yet had a chance to let Libby's story of what had happened sink in. The few details were so sketchy, so fantastic—crazy, crazy Missie Rollins! tunnels! mudslides!—beyond anything she could have imagined. She would have to piece it together again more slowly, more rationally, more sequentially. Then maybe it would finally become real to her.

"Libby, we'll be back just as soon as we can. Tillie is fine. She's got a fever, too, just like you. They're going to fix her foot, and we'll drive right back home with her. We can thank God Jake was there to find her!"

"Who?" Libby said.

"Jake! Jake Charpentier, Libby! You know, Rose's boyfriend. He came back to Indian Meadow just today—" Madeleine stopped. Libby had fallen asleep.

Madeleine sat in Harry Littlefield's big gray Cherokee driving up to Lake Placid. Their conversation had been oddly disjointed. One minute they would speak together in a relaxed companionable way, going over the events of the afternoon, trying to sort out the facts so that they made some sense. And then suddenly they would be overcome by the most profound shyness. It was too soon to speak of what had happened between them at the pond, and yet it dominated their senses. Were Madeleine and Harry to be perfectly honest, they would have had to admit that the intense feeling that had sprung up so suddenly between them now towered in importance above all of the afternoon's calamities, anxieties, disclosures, and heroics.

Obviously they would have felt quite differently had the girls not been safe. Madeleine didn't even want to consider how that might have been. But everything had in fact ended so well! Yes, the girls had suffered. And yes, poor Tillie had probably broken her foot. But what parents haven't, at one time or another, found themselves rushing to the emergency room on behalf of an injured child? All this would surely recede into the past, become a great adventure the girls would both look back on as they grew up.

"I'm glad we're driving up there together, Harry," she said. "After everything that's happened today, I'm not sure I could have managed this trip alone."

"Well, at least the fog's starting to lift. We're making very good time. And there's more room in this car for Tillie to stretch out and go to sleep in the back. . . ." He reached over and caressed her hand, and they remained quiet for several miles.

"You know," she said just as they were getting to the outskirts of Lake Placid, "Libby never said who it was that picked her up. Did you notice?"

"Hmm?"

"All she said was that it was 'some nice person.' That sounded odd, somehow. I mean, who would pick up a little

176

kid, all wet, no shirt, and just drop her off like that without even pulling into the driveway to make sure she got home all right?"

"You're right. It is strange. Wonder who it was? Wonder why they didn't stop?"

It was close to eleven o'clock before everybody came back from Lake Placid. Jake followed Harry and Madeleine in the small pickup he'd borrowed from the Thompsons. Tillie had been so overjoyed to see her mother again, that despite her broken foot and her fever she managed to seem much more like her old self than Libby had. She had so many questions and stories she could barely contain herself: about Libby, about that crazy Missie acting like she was a little girl and playing with them, about the water starting to rise in the tunnel, the rocks all tumbling down just as they were trying to climb up them. And then she regaled them with a blow-by-blow account of Jake's dramatic rescue, complete with musical accompaniment: "There I was, singing 'This Old Man' for like the *twentieth* time. . . !" She didn't settle down and fall asleep in the backseat until, apparently, the painkiller they'd given her at the hospital kicked in at last. She fell asleep talking.

It had been a multiple fracture and a fairly complicated one, at that. They'd been lucky to come to a hospital with a strong emphasis in orthopedics and sports-related injuries. By the time the doctors and nurses were through with her, Tillie was wearing a funny-looking space-age boot on her left foot that would have to stay in place for at least a month. But there would be no complications or permanent damage.

As soon as they got home, they put Tillie down on Madeleine's bed downstairs, elevating her foot as best they could. There were a few cranky, whimpering noises, and then she sank into the pillows and sweet oblivion.

Jake sat at the kitchen table while Rose did the last of the washing up. She was already dressed for bed in a long

177

flannel nightgown. She wanted to hear firsthand how he had followed the path of the creek, how he'd discovered the mudslide, all of it.

"You know, Rose, that creek's shifted course—a lot—since the survey map was done. It's moved to the east. That tunnel, or whatever it was those poor kids were thrown into, well, near as I can tell, it must have been directly in the creek's path. It was just a matter of time. And what with all the flooding we've had on account of the rain, well, I guess those two little girls just got out in the knick of time. They must be some kind of climbers! My hat's off to 'em both." He drank down the last of his Molson's and stood up. Harry Littlefield had just stepped into the room.

"Jake, I thought I'd walk around the place and make sure everything's locked up. Care to join me?"

All the cars were gone except theirs. They walked down toward the toy barn. The lights had been left on and seemed especially bright now that the sky had cleared. Nobody'd been by to turn them off.

"Jake, I want to thank you for doing what you did. You know, I've had this place for more than four years now, and this is the first I ever heard of there being an underground passageway down here. Had you ever heard any talk of such a thing?"

They were at the barn now, walking into it.

"No. Never. It's some kind of surprise, let me tell you. In fact, if I hadn't seen where little Tillie ended up, I never would have believed it. See, they were only half a mile or so from here as the crow flies. But no way could anybody have got to where they came out! Not from here, anyway."

"Except by doing what you did, you mean," Harry said.

"I just thank God I thought of it!"

"We all do, Jake. We all do." By tacit consent, they headed for the steps to the loft. The big cardboard cartons the girls had described so vividly were over to the side of the hatch. Harry found the knothole and lifted up the board. They both looked down.

The light from the opened hatch threw a shimmering rectangle upon the roiling surface of murky black floodwater—risen nearly to the level of the top step. But the sharply angled, pewter-colored patch of illumination did not disclose—though it missed doing so by no more than a matter of inches—the sodden empty-eyed mass that stared up at them unseen in the shadows.

Harry slammed the board down again with a shudder.

"My God, Jake! It's flooded nearly to the top! What am I going to do about that?"

"Well, sir, the way I see it, it'll all still be there in the morning. Lots of the old houses around here have flooded cellars like this all through May and June, and sometimes into July. I've noticed the old-timers don't get too exercised over this kind of thing, and most of those old houses will still be standing after you and me are six feet under. Why don't we wait on this until we've both had a good night's sleep, eh?"

"Jake, you make a damn fine point. I'm with you!" He laughed. He was exhausted! But then, just to make sure, he asked, "You don't think it could rise any *more* do you?"

"Naah, it stopped raining hours ago. If anything, the water level will probably go down some overnight."

One of the searchers apparently had left a ratty old sweater behind on the floor. Harry picked it up without thinking and tossed it onto an open shelf. They turned off the lights in the barn, closed the big front doors, and went off into the clear moonlit darkness. Harry headed straight for his guest cottage. He was too tired to do more than give a fleeting, smiling thought to Madeleine, blowing an airy kiss in her direction as he walked by the house.

And Jake, with all that had already transpired on that day, did not think anybody could possibly object if he just went upstairs and crawled into bed next to Rose. He was right. Nobody did. Least of all Rose.

Once all the lights had gone out, fifteen-year-old Sean Congdon felt it was safe to emerge from behind the laundry shed. He ached all over. He'd been hiding, squished into a corner behind the water heater for so long that he'd actually dozed off for a time.

He couldn't believe the fuss those assholes had made! All he'd done was lift a lousy hundred dollars out of his mother's cash box! You'd've thought he'd committed murder. That jerk Wilbur! Half the town combing the hills for him. It just didn't make sense.

Well, he was out of here now. The sooner the better. Sean stretched his awkward, gangly frame. He walked away from the laundry shed, past the darkened toy barn. Imagine all those creeps out looking for him! It was almost like being famous. Maybe he'd got mentioned on the TV, and never even saw it. Oh well, they'd never have to worry about ol' Sean again. That was for sure.

If the weather hadn't been so bad, he would have been long gone. He'd sneaked out of the house with his mother's money, some clothes, and some food stuffed into his backpack. He was going to cut around the edge of town and hitch a ride out beyond the Stoddard Mountain trailhead. But it had been raining so bad and the visibility was so lousy that he changed his plan and decided to camp overnight in the cruddy old lean-to they had in there.

And that's just what he would have done—until all those lunatics had come crawling through the woods looking for him. He still couldn't figure out why they stopped when they did. He heard the horns honking and knew it was some kind of signal. But he didn't risk moving out of there until he heard the cars finally drive off.

And then, just as he'd hit the road again, he was nearly run over by this gray Cherokee coming at him like a bat out of hell. It had to have been going nearly sixty and only missed hitting him by inches. He about shit in his pants! At least they hadn't spotted him. That's when he decided to wait until the fog lifted before trying again.

He'd been smart to wait. The moon was nearly full, and he could see just fine. He came to a muddy clearing,

180

looked like maybe an old wagon road—two ruts. It probably went to the main road. Sean hung a left.

That's when he saw the BMW—its bright orange paint fairly glowing with promise in the moonlight. Sean didn't actually know how to hotwire a car, but he'd seen it done a couple of times. . . . He peered in the window. Holy shit! The fucking keys were right there! Jesus fucking Christ! Sean Congdon had got lucky at last. He didn't hesitate.

He backed out very slowly. The ground was muddy as shit, and he didn't want to blow this. He'd never even been *in* a car this good, and now here he was driving it! Sean Congdon, having found reverse, now found first, and then second. The car purred into action. He didn't find the lights until he'd gone nearly a mile. Then he found fourth.

And then Sean Congdon left the village of Indian Meadow behind forever.

CHAPTER
20

TIRED as he was, Harry found himself sitting up, wide awake, in the middle of the night. He'd had a terrible nightmare. Short, painful, jagged scenes had played before him like a film it actually hurt to watch. Fragments flashing by with breathless, threatening speed. He'd woken up just to stop the tape from spinning. That's what it had felt like: watching one of those garish, synthesized MTV videos Hillary used to love.

Hillary. And crazy Missie Rollins. Harry was sure that he knew now what had happened to Hillary, and how. Now that he was awake, the images from the dream had managed to organize themselves. He could see it all quite clearly. It was as though he'd actually been there.

Missie entering the barn, catching Hillary by surprise while she'd been alone and intent on preparing an inventory of the barn's contents. Hillary, who hated to be interrupted when she was immersed in one of her projects, would certainly have let her irritation show, would think nothing of saying something cutting and nasty. God knew, she'd been good at that. And she would have been much too self-absorbed to recognize any warning signs about Missie's mental state.

And then? Missie might have been angry or vindictive or threatened. Maybe because Hillary was selling the toys. Missie was obviously fixated in some way about the toy barn. Somehow she'd manipulated Hillary into the underground room. How would she have managed that? How else! By telling her that there were more toys hidden away down there—better, rarer, more valuable toys. Hillary had always been so greedy—for possessions, for excitement, for life—always looking for *more*! Hillary would have swallowed the bait.

And then Missie had trapped her. Just like Libby and Tillie. Only Hillary never got out. Those torrential rains—one of the worst thunderstorms in years—flooding everywhere. There had been a cave-in. These things didn't happen all at once, they happened in stages. The first one had happened while Hillary was down there, probably fighting desperately to find a way out. It was even possible that her own efforts to dig out might have precipitated what followed. Oh, God, Hillary! Poor, elegant, stubborn, greedy little Hillary.

She hadn't slipped and fallen into the creek during the storm. That had been Emmett Wilbur's reconstruction of the scene. Harry had never quite bought it. But now he found he could picture the storm-swollen creek bursting into the tunnel at full force to claim her, picking her up and carrying her off. Just another object in its mindless, roaring path. Oh, God.

He could picture it all too clearly.

Harry paced about the one-room cottage, wishing it weren't the middle of the night, wishing he could call Emmett Wilbur to tell him what he'd figured out. He was so sure he was right, and so horrified. It hurt so much to feel it all again. He wanted to be able to talk to somebody.

He thought of Madeleine. How good it would be to have

her here beside him to tell this to! For a moment, he considered walking over to the house, waking her. He imagined placing his hand on her shoulder—she'd be in a soft silk nightdress, all warm with sleep—to wake her. And then he remembered how they'd put Tillie down on Madeleine's bed. No. He couldn't go there now. He would let the lady sleep. They would have other nights together. Many other nights. It would be morning before he knew it.

By seven o'clock, Harry couldn't wait any longer. Hours had passed since he'd watched the sun come up. He walked through the kitchen door quietly, not wanting to wake anybody. But Rose was up and about, humming cheerfully, making coffee, setting the big table for breakfast. She looked up and nodded at him as he entered, saying good morning in a sweet lilting voice, and then casually set another plate down on the table for him. Harry politely asked permission before picking up the phone and dialing Emmett Wilbur's home number. Mrs. Wilbur answered placidly; they were early risers. Pulling the wire as far as it could go, Harry stepped into the small hallway, his back to Rose, and began—in a very confidential tone of voice—to tell Wilbur the troubling scenario he'd worked out during the night.

Wilbur listened without interrupting. When Harry had finished, he said, "That does sound plausible. Terrible, terrible, but plausible. Poor woman! Must be difficult for you, I'm sure.

"You know, Harry, as soon as I heard that tape your wife left behind, I figured it must have been Missie who'd come in and that she was somehow involved in your wife's death. But I'm not sure we'll ever know how, exactly, unless she decides to tell us herself.

"Another thing: Joe Mitford came 'round late last night, after the girls were found, to tell me about his sister. Apparently she'd taken to roaming about your place most every night. It's where she'd spent her childhood, as I'm sure you know. She's been acting real peculiar since she

184

came back from California . . . leaving the house after she figured Joe and his mother had gone to sleep. But Joe had noticed it and worried about it, so one night last week he took it upon himself to follow her, see where she went. He'd been wrestling with his conscience about it ever since. He came straight over here when he heard about what happened to those little girls.

"We're going to be charging Melissa Rollins tomorrow morning at ten—lawyers and all coming up—at the county sheriff's office. I was planning to call you."

Libby and Tillie had come into the kitchen while Harry was on the phone. He couldn't help but notice that they'd both apparently spent the night on Madeleine's double bed in the front bedroom. Even as he listened to Wilbur talking, part of him remembered what he'd nearly gone and done during the night. Damn smart he'd held back!

"I'll be there, Constable," Harry said and hung up.

"Good morning, Libby, Tillie. How are you feeling today?" he said then.

Tillie had hobbled over to the table and sat herself down, putting her bad foot on the chair next to her. She looked cheerful and happy. Her eyes sparkling, she said, "Did you hear what happened to Libby and me yesterday? It was really scary, like on TV, or something!"

"Yes, Tillie, I was there when your mother picked you up at the hospital last night, remember?"

"Oh! Right! That was you, wasn't it? I guess I was kind of sleepy by then."

"And how about you, Libby?" Harry asked. "Are you all better this morning? Have you got your voice back? Fever all gone?"

Just to make sure, Rose walked over and placed a practiced hand on both girls' foreheads.

Libby let her forehead be felt. Her face wore an odd, puzzled sort of expression.

"It was awful," she said finally, still quite hoarse. "I've never been so scared in all my life. We had to climb out of

185

that place . . . and everything was wet and slippery. All this water kept coming in, and the rocks we were trying to climb up kept moving and slipping. When I woke up this morning I couldn't remember whether it really really happened, or if . . . like, maybe I'd just dreamed it . . . you know? I hurt all over. My throat hurts. I don't feel so good, Rose. Where's Mom?"

Rose searched Libby's pale face. She didn't really look like her old self. Her eyes were dull. Probably still had a low-grade fever. "I'll get you some aspirin, honey."

They heard Madeleine coming down the front stairs.

"Hi, guys." She smiled when she saw everybody. "Looks like you all got up before me. I finally went to sleep in that other upstairs bedroom. That way, I was right above the two of you so I could hear if you needed anything. I never heard a thing. Does that mean you both had a good night's sleep? Hmmm?" She kissed them both good morning. While she was kissing Tillie, her eyes looked up to meet Harry's.

He smiled at her. "Rose seems to have invited me to stay for breakfast," he said.

Madeleine nodded. "Delighted to have you," she said. "That's odd," she added, "I seem to count *six* places."

That's when Jake walked in from outside. He was carrying two bags of groceries. "I went to get milk," he announced. "And you were out of orange juice, too. And I picked up the newspapers. And in honor of the two bravest little girls in the whole world, here's two dozen of the world's very best jelly doughnuts—made fresh this morning by Indian Meadow's own Mrs. Bird. You folks ever tasted these? They're something else!"

The doughnuts—raspberry and apricot and blueberry—were small, light, delicately flavored ovals. Jake had not overstated their merits. Between the six of them, they began to disappear with astonishing speed. Madeleine smiled over at Rose and Jake and realized he must have spent the night. They were a good couple. And there was Harry, sitting across from her, looking at her with those amazing eyes of his! She was still not used to his face. She kept discovering new things about it. This morning she noticed how young he actually was. She didn't know his age, had never thought about it. She loved his face!

She also loved the way they were all sitting here so relaxed together, making pigs of themselves. Yesterday they had turned a corner together. Triumphed over tragedy. And life, this morning, was probably as good as it ever gets. She would remember this clear blue Sunday morning, the six of them sitting around the mellow pine table in this beautiful, limpid mountain light, for the rest of her life.

She had Libby and Tillie back!

Safe and sound.

Harry stood up, stretched his tall, lean frame, and said, with a groan, "Oooph! I ate much too much! That was delicious. Thank you Rose, Madeleine. And Jake, thanks for your generous donation of doughnuts. Uh, I think I'll go check the water level out there. Care to join me?"

Jake stood up and did some stretching and groaning of his own. "Yeah, sure, good idea," he said.

The morning was so clear, the colors so pure and bright, it was hard to believe how this had all looked yesterday. Harry and Jake walked together in comfortable silence, enjoying the air. They reached the toy barn, opened the doors, and walked in.

Once again they raised the lid, and with the lifting of that wooden board, both could immediately feel themselves being drawn back into the clammy, nightmarish, fearful atmosphere that had prevailed the day before.

They peered into the dark pit, into the glistening sheen of black greasy-looking water. It had receded. Several more rough stone steps were now visible to them through the murk. The air that rose up smelled rank, like spoiled vegetation.

"Well, I guess it's gone down some," Harry said, his nose wrinkling. "You know, Jake, I'd like to check out that

187

spot where you found Tillie. See how bad the cave-in is. I'm going to have to do something about all this . . . I don't know what."

"I'll take you out there. Now that I know where it is, we can reach it from the road. Don't have to follow the damn creek all the way up. In fact, did you know that Libby tied her shirt to a branch by the side of the road so we could find Tillie? That's a smart little girl."

"So that's what happened to her shirt. I heard Madeleine asking about it, but Libby didn't say."

The site of the cave-in showed the tunnel had been completely blocked. They could find no sign of where Libby and Tillie might have managed their heroic scramble to safety. Indeed, there was now a kind of raised mound, formed by all the rocks and uprooted trees that had been sucked in by the tumult of the mudslide. Any water down in what was left of the tunnel would probably drain out slowly, seeping gradually back into the soil.

Alas, these conditions did not offer Harry the substantiation he'd been hoping to find. If Hillary had been swept out by the force of the water rushing down through the collapsed tunnel, there was nothing here to prove it. The way things looked now, nobody down there could possibly be swept into the flow of the creek. But it had happened a month ago, and there had been more flooding and another cave-in since. So there really was no reason to rule out his theory.

"Thanks for bringing me up here, Jake. What do you think I should do about all this?"

"Well, there'll be trouble whenever you have flooding, and eventually the barn's foundations could go."

"Yep. I think you're right about that."

"I think the best thing to do would be to fill in the whole damn thing. Close it off, rechannel the stream. Unless you want to move the barn, or maybe sell it. Somebody might want to buy it from you, move it to another site. Seen quite a bit of that going on in these parts lately."

188

"Wouldn't it be a whole lot easier just to throw a bunch of dirt on this and fill it all in?"

"Damn right. Besides, that's a real pretty barn. Be a shame to lose it."

While Harry and Jake were out, Libby and Tillie decided they'd like to set up their boarding school game out on the porch steps. Rose volunteered to help Libby bring in all the dolls and blankets they'd been using. The barn was too far for Tillie to hobble to with her trussed-up broken foot.

"You sure you don't mind coming out here with me?" Rose asked Libby as they walked to the barn.

"Oh, no. It's okay. And I know everything we were using for the game. You wouldn't." But once they'd actually stepped inside, Libby hesitated, doing a rather cautious visual 360-degree sweep. Rose kept an eye on her.

Then the moment passed, and Libby turned to Rose with a smile and said, "It'll be nice to get all this stuff over to the house. We were playing this real good game." She walked briskly over to the loft steps and began to gather up all the toys she could, dumping them into a large doll blanket for carrying. She asked Rose to collect the Shirley Temple paraphernalia that was littered about the area near the steps, including the abruptly abandoned eighteen-inch Shirley herself.

When Rose had bundled all this stuff together, she paused and took a look around. She couldn't help but try to imagine what must have taken place while she and Jake had been, well, had been outside. "Is this the place where the trapdoor is?" she asked, stepping gingerly into the space behind the steps where the boxes were stored.

"Uh-huh." Libby, her face set, her mouth drawn into a thin, straight line, made no move to go near it. Rose backed off, but she couldn't help adding, "I guess you don't want to see it again, do you?"

Libby shook her head no.

"Sorry. Of course you wouldn't." Rose hated herself for being stupid. For a moment, curiosity had simply got the

189

better of her. She went over to Libby and hugged her. Libby's body felt so tense . . . so stiff. The poor thing!

"Now, Libby, you've got nothing to worry about. It's all over. Everything's going to be just wonderful from now on. That crazy old Missie Rollins is going to be put away behind bars where she belongs. Do you understand that?" Rose crouched down and tried to look Libby in the eyes. Was she okay? Did she understand? It was so hard to tell.

Rose decided to let her be.

She bustled around picking up the rest of the dolls. Then she waited quietly by the door for the silent, rigid little figure standing by the steps to rouse herself from whatever it was she was feeling. Which eventually, with a barely perceptible look of puzzlement, she did.

They left the barn together without another word.

CHAPTER
21

THE next morning, the first Monday in July, Harry Littlefield and Jake Charpentier drove to the county seat, where formal charges would be lodged against Missie Rollins. Madeleine and Rose, whose presence was not required, thought it best to stay home with Libby and Tillie. Should the matter come to trial, the girls might be called upon to testify. For the present, depositions taken from them by Constable Wilbur would serve.

Mrs. Mitford had become quite hysterical upon learning of the allegations against her daughter, as one might have expected. But when the pale, passive Missie did not deny the charges, indeed appeared to all intents to confirm them—nodding in meek, hollow-eyed acceptance when Constable Wilbur arrived for her—Pamela Perry Mitford simply took to her bed, where, under heavy sedation, she spent the remainder of the day. Before Missie Rollins actually stepped into the constable's car, she paused to look back at the comfortable Victorian house she was leaving behind. Then she reached into the big straw flower-embroidered handbag she was carrying—a souvenir of Catalina Island—and took out a pair of dark glasses. Her hands trembling just a little, she opened the garish zebra-striped frames and adjusted them carefully on the bridge of her nose. Then she got in. Joe slid in next to her and they drove off without a word.

In the future, Joe would come to look back on this terrible time and realize, rather ruefully, that it had marked—nearly twenty years too late—his coming-of-age.

He did everything that was required, showing compassion to his sister, respect for the law, and behaving, to the best of his ability, with appropriate prudence and maturity. Once the dreadful business was over and done with, Mrs. Mitford would never return to the offices of Lakeshore Realty again. She retired. It was Joe's turn to take over now.

In the matter of Elizabeth and Matilda Rafferty, Melissa Mitford Rollins was charged with several counts of willful and reckless endangerment of minors.

However, based on Harry's and Emmett Wilbur's most recent reconstruction of events, and on facts Joe Mitford was able to supply, in the case of the late Hillary Littlefield, Melissa Mitford Rollins was charged with several counts of reckless endangerment and one count of negligent manslaughter.

Throughout the almost perfunctory, low-key proceedings, she sat cowering next to her brother, dressed in something wrinkled and pink, her scraggly blond-gray hair partially pulled back by a droopy ribbon. They made a peculiar pair. Joe, middle-sized and middle-aged, wearing a neat blue suit, so ordinary and acceptable, really. Until you caught sight of his face and saw those pained, splayed eyes of his seeming to take in both sides of the room at once.

When the charges were read, Missie reached into her handbag and took out a shabby spiral notebook. Then she uncapped a red felt-tipped pen and copied down everything she heard.

Most of those present in the Essex County Courthouse

that morning doubted Missie would ever be considered fit to stand trial.

But if the deeply disturbed defendant were never to speak in her own behalf in a court of law, she had nonetheless been preparing her testimony faithfully for years, storing up each of the pieces of her defense against the day some unknown strangers might read them and make of them what they would. Her notebooks.

And that's what Rose and Madeleine were deep in the middle of when Jake and Harry returned later that afternoon. The kitchen table was piled high with spiral notebooks. They'd both been reading for hours, discovering the clinical Rosetta stone to Missie Rollins's tormented personality. Or, rather, personalities, for there were indeed several. Each with a different handwriting.

"You know, one of the saddest and most ironic things about all this," Madeleine said after they'd shared their discovery with Harry and Jake, "is that one of her personalities—the one who tried to grow up, the one who went out to California and got married—was actually a good writer. She was the person Melissa Rollins wanted to be and almost succeeded in becoming. It's her intelligence that's behind these diaries. Even when she's speaking as the nine-year-old, the girl who was locked in the tunnel by her older sisters all those years ago—the event that must have triggered her illness—the insights and the style of the writing belong to the adult."

"Listen to this." Rose read from a random entry, "'Margot and Elaine were at school, so Mama let me meet the Garden Club ladies today. She said I was her 'mistake' and everybody laughed. But Mrs. Bird said I was a pretty little thing and admired the pink ribbon in my hair. Mama let me have some cocoa. That was nice. But she was cross with me when some spilled on my chin. It was just a drop, but it spoiled everything. I hate Mama!'"

"See," Madeleine said, "it's a nine-year-old's handwriting, but the spelling and punctuation and overall style are

193

too sophisticated for somebody that age. It's as though the grown-up Missie was trying to record, and perhaps exorcise, everything bad that had ever happened to her as a child. Missie didn't even start these notebooks until some time in the late seventies, apparently as part of some therapy or other she'd begun."

"So you think it's all there . . . everything we need to know to get her into a mental hospital?" Harry asked.

Madeleine and Rose both nodded yes vehemently. "I'm no shrink, but it certainly looks that way," Rose said, "and we've only skimmed the surface."

"What I can't understand," Harry said, "is how the fact of that tunnel could have been hidden all these years. When I bought this place, there was no mention of it. I mean, everybody knew it had originally been built by Quaker abolitionists and that it had once been a station on the Underground Railway, but not a word about the tunnel. I mean, I spent a lot of time in that barn when I first moved in, looking through that amazing toy collection, and it was obvious there was no cellar to the place. It's a packed-earth floor. That wooden part by the hayloft steps . . . well, it just seemed like a support for the steps. It never occurred to me. I can't help but feeling that I should have known . . . that I could have prevented—"

"Don't! Don't think like that, please!" It wrenched Madeleine's heart to see what he was thinking.

"Harry," Rose said. "I've lived here all my life and I didn't know. My mom *worked* here, for heaven's sakes! They used to let me play in the toy barn all the time. *Nobody* knew about it. It was a secret the oldest boy discovered. Locking a younger kid down there was like an initiation rite. After all, there were six of them all told. Only when Margot and Elaine did it to little Missie, they screwed up. Instead of letting her out a few minutes later, their mother called them away on some errand. Missie was left alone down there in total darkness for hours and hours. When they finally came back late that night to rescue her, they were so worried about being found out, they swore her to secrecy. Concocted a story about a curse and made her sign an oath in blood . . . the whole bit. They told her that her parents would die if she ever told anybody."

Madeleine took up the story. "By then, the damage had been done. Poor fragile Missie had been the butt of so many cruel pranks. This one was the final straw. It broke her spirit. Not that those sisters of hers noticed. And instead of being welcomed back and comforted after her terrifying ordeal, she was severely punished for being so thoughtless as to try to run away from home."

"The prank was never repeated," Rose put in. "Missie never told. The older kids went off to prep school and college. I don't think I ever met any of them. Then the Mitfords sold the place. Joe, as the youngest, never heard about any of it, but he was always protective of Missie. He knew there was something . . . he just didn't know what."

They sat there in silence for a time. Libby came in and asked, "What's everybody so quiet about?" Madeleine reached out to her, and lifted her on her lap.

"We were just sitting here thinking, sweetie. Thinking how lucky we all are to be here together. And how much we all love you."

Libby laughed. "Yeah, sure, I'll just bet!" she said, good-naturedly letting herself be hugged and fussed over. "So since you love me so much, I guess getting some cookies won't be a problem, huh? Tillie wants some, too."

"Coming right up," Rose said, getting up from the table and walking over to the cupboard.

They decided the constable should have the notebooks. Since Rose and Jake were planning to go into the village anyway, they volunteered to take them.

When they'd gone, Madeleine turned to Harry and said, "Harry, I've never seen it. That trapdoor. The steps going down. I don't know, I think I should. In order to put it all behind me."

"I was planning to check on the level of the water, anyway. We can go now if you want."

When they got to the toy barn, Madeleine hesitated. "God, I don't know. Suddenly this seems like a really scary thing to do."

"It is. It's awful. I'm having the whole thing filled in. Making damn sure nobody ever gets trapped down there again."

Harry moved both cartons. Madeleine stood aside, watching him. She'd heard about those cartons, had heard about this hidden-away place behind the steps many times now. But seeing it was different. He lifted the lid, found the hook, and attached it through the knothole. She moved in next to him and they both looked down.

It was so dark, at first her eyes couldn't see anything at all. Then she discerned the faint glimmer of water, now some ten or twelve feet down.

And then they were almost overpowered by the strong odor that rose up from the pit. A terrible sick, sweet, noxious stench.

Harry dropped the lid down with a bang.

"Oh! That was horrible!"

"Must have been some animal," he said, shaking his head in pity and revulsion. "Let's get out of here, Madeleine. It's over."

CHAPTER

22

ONE week later, Madeleine was driving back from the village with a full load of groceries in preparation for Matt and Sylvie's visit the next day. They were planning to stay a week. She was wondering whether she ought to have tried to tell them more about all that had happened. The fact was, she had tried, several times, and had failed. And they'd been so excited about coming up to see her, talking about books they'd found on the Adirondacks, day trips they were planning.

She could just picture what they were expecting. Probably very much what she'd had in mind when she'd taken the place over the phone from Joe Mitford all those weeks ago. A kind of woodsy, rustic cliché: pure air, gorgeous views, healthy simplicity. Almost true, at that. Well, let them get up here, let them all sit around, relaxed, with drinks in their hands—she'd bought Tanqueray's, quinine water, limes—and one way or another, the story would get itself told. She smiled. Explaining Harry Littlefield's presence in her bedroom would probably be as good a place to start as any.

After she'd gone a mile or two, the road just ahead was blocked by an enormous yellow Caterpillar earth-moving machine, inching its way slowly up the steep incline off to the left of the road. Jake Charpentier, looking very competent and professional in neat olive drab coveralls and a bright orange hard hat, was directing the driver. She slowed down and came to a stop. When the maneuver was completed, Jake walked over to her car. He poked his head down to speak to her through the open window.

"I found something for you, Madeleine," he said.

"Oh, yes?"

He reached into his back pocket and tugged at what she had supposed to be a bright bandanna draped, in the prevalent woodsman's fashion, to dangle luxuriantly.

"It's Libby's shirt. The one she tied to a tree that day to mark where Tillie was." Madeleine reached out the window for it, holding it briefly to her cheek.

"Jake. Thank you! That's great. She'll get a kick out of this, I'm sure." It was stiff, wrinkled, and very dry; the weather had been exceptionally fine for quite some time. Madeleine put the faded raspberry-colored sweatshirt down on the seat beside her and, with a cheerful wave to Jake, drove on up the road.

Rose had gone to Vermont. She was coming back that evening with her three children, and she and Jake were setting up temporary housekeeping in an apartment in the village. Then they would buy their brand-new, long-awaited twenty-four-foot mobile home. Madeleine and Rose had agreed upon a new three-day-a-week schedule for her job at the Perry house.

Harry had been baby-sitting while she'd been away. He seemed very grateful for her return.

"Hi, you," they said to each other fondly, caressingly, in the insatiable, rather fatuous way of new lovers.

But then Harry had to leave, as she'd fully expected. She

knew he'd been crazy with impatience to get down and watch his earth-moving project. He would be down there with Jake and his crew for the rest of the afternoon.

So then it was just the three of them again. The first time in a long time. Tillie and Libby helped her unload the groceries, and when they were finally done—there'd been ten bags!—Madeleine remembered Libby's shirt. She got it from the car and brought it in.

Libby's response was disappointing.

"Hey," Madeleine said as she handed it to her, "remember this?"

But it was Tillie who ran—hobbled—up to it excitedly, saying, "Oh, look, Libby, the shirt you had on when we excaped!"

"That's *es*-caped," Libby corrected loftily, sounding annoyed. She took the shirt, gave it a cursory uninterested glance, and threw it down on a chair.

"Well, *ex*-cuuu-se me!" Tillie replied in a highly offended tone. And rather cleverly, Madeleine thought. Then both girls left the kitchen and went back to the front porch and whatever ongoing game they were engrossed in this week.

So now she had the house entirely to herself. She made herself a cup of tea and took it into the living room. The afternoon sun was pouring in. The quiet, mellow room reminded her of that day they'd arrived, seeing it the first time. How she'd absolutely loved this place from that very moment.

In spite of how desperate she'd been! Running away from Gil. Alone in this strange distant place, halfway up a mountain. What could she have been thinking of? For a time, it had seemed she'd left one kind of horror behind in New York just to be swept into something even worse in Indian Meadow.

And yet . . . somehow, she'd come out the other side. She'd got incredibly lucky. She'd stumbled into the very happiness she'd wondered about so wistfully when they'd stopped at that overlook on the thruway. Happiness that just was, that you didn't have to work for every minute. *Love!* She'd fallen in love. And Harry loved her, too. They were crazy about each other! Now, who could have expected that?

During the last week, without saying anything to Harry, she'd gathered up her courage and dialed Gil's number in New York . . . several times. But all she ever got was that assinine recorded message. "Away on an assignment," indeed! She didn't care anymore. Let him be far, far away— the farther away the better.

She and Harry would work that all out. All in good time. They had their whole lives before them. Winters in New York. Summers up here. Writing books. Of course, there would be difficulties. But they'd face them together. Right now, she was blissfully content. She drank the last of her tea and put the cup down, listening to the comfortable ticking of the old clock on the mantel. She'd spent years learning what it was like to be unhappy. To grit your teeth, to get through and survive at all costs. Now was her time to learn to be happy. She'd paid her dues.

She could see Tillie and Libby playing on the porch from where she sat. Could hear the muted babble of the different voices they assumed as they portrayed the characters in their game. Tillie wore that orthopedic shoe of hers with such good grace. She'd really grown, become more independent, more of a person in her own right, since they'd come here.

Libby. Well, Libby wasn't quite out of the woods yet. She'd grown more inward, less spontaneous, since that awful day they were trapped. But seeing her now, playing so contentedly with her sister in the dappled sunlight on the big porch, well, surely time would take care of whatever might still be troubling her.

Just then, as though she'd been able to hear her mother's thoughts, Libby looked up. It was such a peaceful, pretty afternoon. Libby felt it and was enjoying it. She caught her mother's glance and smiled winningly at her. Mommy was

200

neat. She loved her a lot. And Rose. And Jake. And Harry, too. Everything was really neat. Except . . .

Except for not remembering. She didn't seem to be able to remember anything about that day they escaped from the caved-in tunnel. Once in a while she'd get a fleeting, distant picture. Like, she seemed to be able to remember getting picked up on the road by some nice person. Sitting in a nice warm car after she'd been very wet and cold and scared. But she couldn't hold on to that picture for more than a tiny second before it left her. Everything she knew about that day came from things she'd been able to pick up from Tillie.

Not remembering made her feel dumb. Like maybe Tillie was suddenly the older one. Just to prove to herself that wasn't true, she grabbed a toy from Tillie's hand.

"Hey! No fair, Libby, that's mine!" the outraged Tillie screamed right on cue. That made Libby feel better.

Yes, Madeleine decided, smiling to herself when they'd quieted down again, as she knew they would. It was just a question of time.

And then the soothing sound of the ticking clock lulled her to sleep.

Three weeks later, down in New Orleans, a shiny black BMW 2002 was being loaded onto the deck of a Panamanian freighter bound for Barranquilla, Colombia. The identifying numerals etched into its engine block had been permanently altered, and it had been supplied with entirely new registration papers.

When the pretty orange car, sputtering and emitting thick blue-black smoke, had hobbled into the all-night garage on the outskirts of Boston very early one Sunday morning, its nervous young driver seemed more than happy to accept the seventy-five dollars, no questions asked, offered him for it by the understanding mechanic.

By the time this lucky mechanic stumbled across the secret stash of cocaine in the trunk, the youth had long since hopped on the T for downtown Boston.